I0691371

Two is for You

Bobby Williams

Published by Open Books

Copyright © 2015 by Bobby Williams

All rights reserved. No part of this book may be reproduced,
scanned, or distributed in any printed or electronic form without
permission except in the case of brief quotations embodied in
critical articles and reviews.

Original image "Ice Storm 2" Copyright © Ross Griff,
licensed under CC BY 2.0 at
https://creativecommons.org/licenses/by/2.0/

Learn more about the artist at
https://www.flickr.com/photos/rossaroni/

ISBN: 069240581X
ISBN-13: 978-0692405819

For under your influence death is inconceivable:
On walks through winter woods, a bird's dry carcass
Agitates the retina with novel images,
A stranger's quiet collapse in a noisy street
Is the beginning of much lively speculation,
And every time some dear flesh disappears
What is real is the arriving grief; thanks to your service,
The lonely and unhappy are very much alive.
-W.H Auden

1

*W*ell...here you are darling, so special. Now take a look at *that* house, go ahead—it's nasty. Mold covered shutters, the whole front porch warped, crabgrass and mud. Isn't it sick? You just know the inside smells bad. Such a sad little tree recently planted there in the front. Looks like a tiny Christmas tree that could only shelter miniature presents and is likely serviced by a dwarf Santa who, if we're being kind, has less need for cookies and fits easily down the chimney. But that's far off, it's only fall. Some people refer to this season as autumn. And when they're using that word it sounds like they're yawning or commenting on a pleasant breeze, oh autumn. These are people who go out picking pumpkins and apples and while doing so discuss seasonal flavors of coffee. The word "autumn" has never been used in *that* house, the Salaznek house.

"Marky, whatcha doing up there?" Mrs. Salaznek yelled upstairs.

"Just reading Ma," replied Mark Salaznek.

"Mmmm, such a smart boy," Mrs. Salaznek said to herself. "I'm goin' out to get more wood for the fire," she yelled to Mark. Her wool socks were bunched below jeans that didn't quite reach her ankles. She stretched the socks up to their full height, tucking the jeans inside. She laced her brown hiking boots over the whole package and stood up from a terribly beige and disastrously worn couch. How worn is this disaster, you're asking? If you were to squat down like inspector doggy on all fours in front of the couch, the two outer cushions would appear to be grinning yellow foam at you. The fabric had burst under the pressure of a decade of butts like two sore blisters and particularly, the foam-smile on the left was missing a few teeth. You see, when Mr. Salaznek, *Richard* Salaznek that is, sits on that couch he likes to have drinks. He's a sad nervous train conductor so as he's drinking he sticks his long arm down between his legs and picks and picks at the foam, for comfort. Sometimes he flicks the pieces at their cats and laughs when the cats cough the foam balls out days later, mumbling "stupid cats," at the poor creatures. Nobody sits on the middle cushion, because in a family of three it never comes into play. Families who don't say autumn are also families who do not sit all three to a three-cushion couch. The middle cushion and backrest are supreme, but their supremacy only serves to alert rare visitors how *disastrously* worn the other sides are. Mark had often considered chainsawing away the sides and repurposing that middle piece into a brand new chair to save the family from embarrassment, but his Mom always looked at the couch and said, "I love this old dirty couch," so he left it.

The front door creaks when she closes it behind her. Her boots pound across the damp porch and down the front steps—she smiles at the cute Dwarf Alberta Spruce she planted two weeks ago. She frowns at the telephone wires slithering into view at the end of the driveway. "The black vipers", as she referred to them, were not dysfunctional as far as the telephone company was concerned, and being that they were technically on private (not town) property, there wasn't anything they were going to do about it—they'd stopped taking her calls last year.

Mrs. Salaznek approached the tree and ran her palm along its dense prickly needles, a mothering touch to the tree's infant cheek. "Mmmm, you smell *so* nice today," she told it, still looking at the black vipers. Two neighbors power-walked by: "Hi, Claudia." They waved without looking, checked their watches, then scuffled along making sure to avoid the black vipers. "Yep," Claudia replied, still rubbing the tiny Spruce.

Mrs. Salaznek left the little Spruce and went to her backyard where she kept her woodpile. She took pride in this pile. She marked the date of the September equinox on her calendar every fall, and on that date would drive to the lumberyard with her chainsaw seatbelted into the back seat. The night before the equinox she'd open all the windows in that crappy house so she could wake up with the smell of wet leaves in her nostrils. She'd make a big breakfast for her son with thick Canadian bacon and call up to him when it was ready, "Marky, come on and eat," and then, "today's the equinox, you wanna come and get some wood with yer Mother or what?" The best days were when he came with her. They'd chainsaw that shit all day long screaming out praise to one another over the rickety motor and through borrowed aviation headphones. They'd wear black and red flannel shirts, matching brown boots. Claudia always wrapped a tight red bandana around her freckled forehead to compliment her tough orange hair— years when Mark couldn't make it he'd surely be home from school in time to unload the wood and help construct the neat backyard pile. Every single year Claudia Salaznek invited her neighbors to help themselves to her wood, but no one ever showed. Finally she put a sign in the front yard: "Free Wood"—with an arrow pointing to the woodpile. The sign only lasted two nights before vandals turned the arrow into an erection forcing her to uproot and discard the kindness into the coveted fireplace.

When Rick got home that night he noticed the sign and asked, "What's with the burnin' boner?"

"I'll throw a second Dick in there if yer not careful," replied Claudia.

Mark looked up from his book to laugh.

"See Marky, that's what you get for trying to be nice," Rick said, another of his classic anti-lessons.

Claudia stacked the front porch three logs at a time preparing for a fire that would heat their home through the night. Mark watched her do it from his window upstairs. He watched her boots plod along the worn path from porch to pile. He smirked at her jeans tucked into the wool socks and the way her stiff ponytail met the back of her head like a stake.

More power-walkers gliding by the driveway, checking their watches: "Hi Claudia," one said, stopping. Claudia Salaznek laid a bulky three-stack down in the yard and veered from the worn path. "Cheryl, Karen, how are we today?"

"We're good...we're goooood," replied Cheryl, checking her watch while looking down at the black vipers lying between them. The two power-walkers huffed and puffed a bit and wiped pellets of sweat from their foreheads. "We were just wondering..."

"Yeah," said Claudia.

"Well, you know, we were just wondering when you were gonna do something about these *wires*. They're a real eyesore."

Mrs. Salaznek blew a plume of frustrated laughter through her eyelashes. "I've been calling the phone company for a year, not much more I can do."

"Okay, we were just curious. It's just that we get nervous about them when the kids are out playing...and with Halloween right around the corner and all..." Karen spoke for Cheryl, and presumably, other neighborhood mothers.

"Then tell them to stay away. I told you before, the

4

phone company says it's private property—nothing they can do."

"All right, Claudia, okay, we were just wondering."

They power-walked, again, on down the road—sharp elbows flying to the side, a terrible winged warning to the casual walker. They checked their pace on their watches and spoke loudly over accelerated autumn heart rates and hard-working lungs. "I bet she hasn't called once, huff-huff-huff. I don't see how they can let their house just *deteriorate* like that, huff-huff-huff."

Claudia returned to the task at hand. Shaking her head, frustrated, she'd actually thought that maybe her neighbors were stopping by for some free firewood. A chilly mist drifted down—she enjoyed the sound of the droplets plopping on all the unraked leaves. An evil grin spread over her face at the thought of Karen and Cheryl's soggy sweaters. Serves 'em right...

Mrs. Salaznek then arrived at a mammoth piece of wood too large for the fireplace. She felt in the proper mood for a bit of chain sawing so she went into the garage, grabbed the metal beast and revved it up. This got Mark's attention upstairs. It disturbed his reading. He could see the rain sliding down his window and wondered what the hell she was up to now? He watched as his mother applied the chainsaw to the thick log. Woodchips sprayed everywhere, the blood and guts of lumber—fine smelling—thank God Mrs. Salaznek was wearing her safety goggles.

As Claudia made her way through the first woodgirth-reducing cut, a married couple of power-walkers stopped by the driveway to observe her work. They checked their watches, huffing and puffing the husband yelled, "CLAUDIA," though she could easily hear him now that the saw had completed its first cut.

"What is it Patrick?"

"WHATCHA DOIN' THERE?" Pat asked, cleverly.

"Just chopping wood," Claudia replied, moving her safety goggles to her forehead.

Patrick and his wife, Patricia, approached the woodpile. Claudia left the chainsaw idling and put her hand out to shake.

"What can I do for you, Patrick?"

"Well..." Patrick began.

"We were just thinking, you know?"

"Yeah?"

"Halloween is right around the corner, and we were just thinking, maybe you could get those wires removed or covered up before the kids go out trick-or-treating."

"You were thinking that?"

"Yeah, kind of..."

"Okay, sure, Pat, I'll do something about it," replied Claudia, firing up her chainsaw more or less in their faces.

"Oh *my*," Patricia jumped backward, shocked by the horrendous mechanical growl.

Mrs. Salaznek once again put her safety goggles over her eyes and called to her son, "WATCH THIS MARKY." She walked not around but directly through the married couple. Patricia had put both of her hands over her small pale mouth. Rain soaked her blonde hair and revealed brown roots. Patrick had his arm around her shoulders for protection as they watched Claudia Salaznek march to the end of her cracked and rutted, stone driveway in her brown hiking boots. "Yeah, I'll do something about it," she told herself. Mark stared at the whole scene from his bedroom window. He knew his mother had no patience for judgmental neighbors. He also knew how fed up she'd become with the black vipers being discussed up and down the block and at dinner parties they'd not been invited to.

Claudia hoisted the chainsaw over her head, a Halloween salute, and brought it down onto the wires and the driveway—small pebbles ricocheted painfully off her gnashing teeth. Her goal was to render the vipers dysfunctional and also to reposition them on public land, thus forcing the hand of the telephone company. Goal one was achieved almost instantly. Claudia was quite pleased at how quickly the chainsaw shredded the rubber insulation and split the sparking wires inside. The wires snapped in half and recoiled to either side of the driveway like the parting of a demon sea, though they did remain firmly on Salaznek property. Well, now I'm gonna have to do something about *that*, thought Mrs. Salaznek.

"HOW'S THAT?" she yelled to Patrick.

"Oh *my*," inserted Patricia.

Patrick looked at his wife, "Let's go..."

Mark shook his head from the window.

"Where the hell are you going?" Claudia called.

"You people are *crazy*," Patricia said, checking her watch.

"Crazy?"

"You're nuts," Patrick said, "look at your house. It's a mess."

"*We're* crazy?" Mrs. Salaznek walked toward them with her chainsaw drawn. "You're not gonna take any firewood with you?" This seemed more a threat than polite invitation.

She laid the idling chainsaw at their feet and walked over to one of the split wires and grabbed it with both hands. Now, Claudia Salaznek began to gyrate sensationally and make peculiar gurgling noises with her mouth.

But first a very brief history of Claudia Salaznek, merry prankster extraordinaire: The April Fools' legend begins with the coincidental unification of April 1st and Easter. Mrs. Salaznek thought she'd dress up as the Easter bunny to entertain her only son. But like most of her pranks, the execution was abysmal and to the point of being dangerous. You see, she couldn't tell Rick her plans because he was an idiot, and even six-year-old Mark could get a straight read on him. He gave everything away. Like that Christmas when he dressed up as Santa but forgot to wear different boots or disguise his voice—"You're not Santa," Mark said, immediately. Angry at having been outsmarted by such a young boy, Rick struck back with, "That's because Santa isn't even real." So, that Easter, Claudia felt compelled to make her son believe in at least one magical holiday mascot.

Rick and Mark sat coloring hardboiled eggs at the kitchen table with some Bobby Dylan playing in the background—pops sipping a cocktail, occasionally rubbing his son's head, son dunking the eggs, giggling like a child, Oshkosh overalls, all's quiet, calm and dark outside—a real Rockwell. Out of nowhere a six-foot-tall rabbit with a crooked one-off look on its face appears in the window and starts hammering the glass two feet from the table. She doesn't even wave—just bangs on the window five times so the glass is quaking— she's trying to reinforce the fact that *this* holiday mascot is very real, but the action manifests itself like an attempted break-in. Mark screams. He doesn't know what to make of this monster. He drops his pretty pink egg on the floor and knocks the bowl of food coloring over as he scrambles away from the table. The coloring slides across the table and drenches his father's pants. As Rick tries (and fails) to save the bowl of food coloring he drops his cocktail on the ground, which adds to the cacophony. The sweet shattering symphony scares the living shit out of young Mark.

Rick gets pissed and shouts, "That stupid bitch," as he wipes helplessly at his pink crotch.

"What? What was *that*?" the child yells, tears on his face.

The Bunny hops away. Still screaming son flees to his room.

"Mother-*fucker*," Rick yells, wiping at his pants. Claudia enters through the front door a few minutes later, having discarded the costume. Her son is inconsolable—this was the end of Easter in the Salaznek house.

A few months later Claudia wanted to make up for that one. It had been a hot July, boy, in the triple digits—Mrs. Salaznek, teacher and champion of the autistic, had her summers off and with her son at camp thought about a fresh prank. What she came up with wasn't as fresh as it was beyond traditional, and once again poorly executed— the old bucket of water over-the-door ambush. She had the initial setup okay—a bowl filled with ice cold water. Everything thereafter was the problem. First, she did not rig the bucket with strings designed to dump and suspend, but instead simply let the bucket rest atop the slightly open front door—between the door and the wall. She sat in the hallway and waited for her son with one of those boombox-like camcorders resting on her shoulder, VHS loaded up and rolling—Action: having just rode his bicycle all the way home from camp, young Mark was sweating about as much as a child can sweat (though a child never cares or feels uncomfortable). The first deluge of freezing water did feel pleasant and refreshing, but when the metallic bucket came crashing down on his forehead that initial joy quickly washed away. The camcorder slammed to the ground along with the bucket, and her son. You can *just* see Claudia running to Mark in the bottom corner of the frame. Add to these two catastrophes countless runs at the ketchup packet as neck-blood trick, gallons of fake vomit, slamming the breaks and screaming as Marky napped during a long car ride and you can understand why no one came running to help but just watched as Mrs. Salaznek wiggled away there in the yard.

Perhaps years of good-natured pranks had come home to roost. Perhaps Mark, Patrick and Patricia were just dazzled by the frenetic front lawn tap dance—she did look kind of funny, after all. The sheer volume of foamy saliva pouring over Claudia's lips did finally confirm, to everyone's horror, that this was no joke.

"Oh *my*," said Patricia. "Patrick, *DO* something," she yelled.

"HELP," yelled Patrick, cleverly.

Mark continued to watch from his window. You can't ever know how someone will react when real life explodes in his face. Most folks will just live and die without ever witnessing a family member in a life or death situation. There's also a ninety-five percent chance that you won't discover a dead body with twisted limbs and a thick, unmistakable stench, and a look that even though rigor mortis has set in still appears to be begging for help. It's also highly unlikely someone will ever point a gun at your forehead with clear intent to fire. You won't ever get knifed, for instance. And no matter how *serious* you believe your life to be, you can't predict what will go through your mind when this type of shit's going down.

It's still on our property, was Mark's first thought. And he still held his book open on his lap. He hoped that this whole thing wasn't as serious as it seemed, but couldn't ignore the noxious foam bubbling from her gums. Even from inside the house he could tell she was gurgling. Her shaking body collapsed to the damp earth as a fire truck, ambulance and police cruiser blazed down the road, squealing and skidding to diagonal halts. Shouting from all directions, "MA'AM, DROP THE WIRE." Neighbors lingered on porches, leering at the chaotic scene—quaint Patricia completely unable to remove her two precious porcelain hands from her mouth, oh my.

"Jimmy, get that fucking axe," yelled an officer.

Mark came running from the front door as the blue uniformed officer lifted the axe into the air and with a hulking grunt chopped down impressively, severing the wire a few feet away from Claudia's grip. Her body went limp. Mark's stiffened. It had grown cold and he hadn't remembered his jacket.

"This your Mother?" the officer asked.

"Yeah...yes sir."

Two paramedics, quickly and carefully, loaded Claudia Salaznek onto a stretcher and into the back of an ambulance. Mark heard one of them say, "I've got a pulse here," and really did hope that meant his *mother's* pulse.

Officer Gerard buckled Mark into the passenger seat of his cruiser. Patrick and Patricia watched this from the Salaznek property, hoping it would soon be over so they could get inside and dry off. Across the street, the Jones's stood on their porch, their three children (two girls and a boy) looked out the front window with their small hands supporting their chins. A few blocks away Karen and Cheryl were huffing and puffing with their elbows out wide, checking their watches, sipping water bottles and wondering what in the hay is all that commotion? The ambulance and police cruiser blew past them at such a raging speed you'd never believe the amount of leaves tossed into the air, very inconvenient, sticking all over their already damp sweaters.

"What could have happened?" Karen wondered aloud.

"Current ripped through her entire left side like a flame to tissue paper," Dr. Engelberger told Mark. "Nothing you could have done, son. The charge was probably eight or nine milliamps, definitely above the let go limit." The doctor looked down at a chart, then back up at Mark, "That's why she kept holding on like that."

"Okay," Mark said.

"She'll be fine...probably a good bit of nerve damage and a long road rehabbing, but she'll live."

2

"What, you don't like porn now?"

"It isn't that."

"Then what?"

"It's mean, Marco."

"Why?"

"You're just watching it because of the receptionist. You *do* think it's funny that none of them have jobs anymore, don't you?"

"She has a great ass."

"That's not an answer."

"I gave *you* a job, didn't I?"

"Also not an answer."

"Why don't you give *me* a job?" Marco Salazar nods toward his morning erection. On the big white movie screen in front of his kingly bed a receptionist does bend over way more than necessary to answer a telephone. Her office attire is so far beyond business casual that it might be considered criminal. Marco likes what she's wearing and this particular actress's ass. The delightful atmosphere provides an added punch in his shorts this morning.

"Come on," he says to his executive assistant, Lana. He pulls a thick black strand of hair away from his eyes, as he looks deep into hers. Marco Salazar's eyes are brown and give the impression of a warm cave. His brow hangs way over like a brim, and makes them seem even more set back, or deep, or engaging, than they really are. He blinks his long eyelashes at Lana for sweet effect. His ears are misshapen and sharp, they lean back and point like a wolf's and it's impossible for him to make a joke other than dry—he looks too serious and polished to spend a single second goofing around.

"Come on," he repeats, adding, "please."

It is precisely 7:17am and downstairs a coffee maker has commenced its daily dripping, gurgling to life with no one around or having been around for twelve hours— these *things*, they're all coming to life and no one seems to care. When Marco purchased the property in Old Brookville he told his clipboard carrying interior designer that he wanted his kitchen to feel *and* operate like a spaceship.

So that's just what happens. Just before the first of every month his dietician arrives at the home in Old Brookville to preprogram the spacefridge computer to communicate with a computer in the local market that tells a whole squadron of human employees what things need to be delivered to Marco's house for the next month. His dietician is the closest thing to a friend Marco has and is always telling him, "You're looking *good* baby, guuuuuuuuuuuuuuh-*UD*. Are you making the shakes like I showed you? Yeah? Okay, good. And what about that salmon with bronze fennel? When I saw it on the screen last month I almost shit myself. Ummm, no, oh my god, that was *duck*, Marco. Yes, I see—no it's not *weird*," and all this time the dietician jab-jab-jabs his fingers at the screen.

"That was so fucking good," Marco tells Lana.

"Are you gonna make me take the train in again?"

"Yes."

"You really suck, Marco. Why?"

"You know why."

"You're the boss, it doesn't matter."

"It matters for *you*. They won't respect you if they know we're fucking."

"Fucking?"

She's putting her clothes on now, which Marco also enjoys. They both know he's lying—everyone on the Egostatistical team already dislikes Lana and it has nothing to do with their impression of her relationship with the company's founder. It's just that she's extremely beautiful and also extremely smart and confident. She's a self-starter able to work individually or in a team atmosphere. She has solid planning, scheduling, and prioritization skills, she's detail oriented. She's professional with way above average verbal communication skills. She functions well in the high-paced, pressure-packed, results-driven environment.

"They already dislike me, Marco. And it's not because we *fuck*, as you say. It's because you make me tell them what to do all the time," Lana says, smartly.

"You're better at it than I am."

"You're terrible at kissing ass."

He continues to watch her dress. She bounces up and down into her work slacks. She'd brought the change of clothes with her in an overnight bag, though there was no room for her car in any of Marco's six garages.

"Marco."

"Yeah?"

"I'm not coming over here again until you get the rest of her stuff out. It's too weird."

"Okay."

The smell of spacebrewed coffee worked its way through the foyer, up and around and around the decadent spiral staircase before sifting through a massive crystal chandelier on its way into the master bedroom.

Marco gets out of the bed and admires his shirtless physique. He runs his palm down from his chest over the abs region and into his CK shorts, dexterously admiring himself.

"See you in a few, boss." Lana smiles, winks.

"You got it."

"Oh, and please don't say anything to the protestors today."

"You mean those pieces of shit?"

"That's really *not* funny."

On her way out Lana took what she knew to be Marco's favorite coffee mug and filled it. She added some spectacular pumpkin flavored cream from the spacefridge. The orange mug said "The Universe knows" on one side and "Believe in yourself" on the other. She felt proud to know that despite being the hottest young software man on earth Marco Salazar could be a corny and sentimental sweetie.

Said sweetie strolls oh so slowly down his spiral staircase—rubbing his palm flat against the abs with every step. At the bottom of the staircase, in the foyer, he pulls a wad of hair to the back of his head while checking the status of his underarm odor, or in this case, lack there of—though there remains a faint sex fragrance running through the house. This house, by the way, is actually a mansion. His neighbors' mansions all have names that sound like Saddlewood Manor or Stone Manor or Avebury Manor and you would *not* be surprised if you saw children riding ponies around the yard all day long.

Marco looks at his cupboard and snickers at the spot where his prized mug used to be. The first gift he ever received from his ex-fiancé, "Well, I guess Lana is gonna get started on removals herself," he says. This is not surprising, considering Lana's self-starting nature. He grabs a bland mug, fills it with spacebrew and flips on the news. This is a daily ritual as his best high school pal, Stone DeFoné, is indeed the local meteorologist.

Stone is a combed and hyper hurricane of a human. His weather forecasting technique is best described as threatening—he's got something against weather. Something even more than the rest of us...

"*Look*, Long Island," he begins, lunging at the lens, his face far too close for comfort, "I've got some bad news." He retreats to the big blue screen, which displays a map of the eastern U.S.A. "What you see here is a winter warm front. A *moist* winter warm front—and it's huge..." His arms flair and flay about the screen like he's spray painting, "...and this normally wouldn't be the worst thing in the world, just your standard messy mix. But as you can see, surface temperatures will be dropping to single digits starting this evening, and will continue to cool Friday morning and into the weekend."

"What's all this mean, Stone," injects the female anchor, her stressed, disheveled hair poking stiffly from her head like yarn, her lobster red business suit desperate to distract from the disastrously dry overworked do.

"Well, Umi, it's ice. We may have another Glaze Event on our hands."

"It can't be worse than ninety-eight's, can it?"

"Ninety-eight, well, it's too early to tell, Umi. Back to you," he points.

"Are we going to get our fun fact for the day?" asks the male co-anchor.

But Stone is gone... The camera points at where he normally stands during the forecast but the monitor reveals only a shot of the map.

"Well, I guess he's cancelled it," chuckles the male co-anchor. "Clearly, this is no time for fun facts."

Stone was uncharacteristically shaken by the question concerning the legendary ice storm of ninety-eight: "Helga," as it was called, and Marco Salazar knows why. Everyone that grew up in that nasty Patchogue neighborhood knows why.

"That fucking bitch. What the fuck? What the *fuck*?" Stone asks the writers in the writers' room. He's hyper again. Spinning like a hurricane he flings his dapper blue and so *slightly* pinstriped suit into the corner, on the floor, purposefully avoiding landing it on a chair.

"We specifically told her not to bring it up Mr. DeFoné. We did *not* put that on-screen, she went off-script."

Two frightened interns and three aggravated writers watch the meteorologist push his fingers through his hair and blow out aggressive air all over the room as he paces. "I mean, doesn't she know I lost my father in that fucking storm?"

"He's de—" one of the interns begins to ask. The writer next to him kicks his ankle, hard, under the table, and puts her hand over his arm, whispers the word, "Don't."

"Listen," Stone says, "I gotta get out of here for a while. I'll be back around four to prep for the evening news. If that front stays on track, we're going to need the Skytracker and Triple Doppler radar."

"Holy shit," one of the interns says.

Stone blazes for the door, and as he exits he turns and points at the intern, "Holy shit is right," he says, and slams the door behind him.

"So, what the hell was that?"

The head-writer stands up, "You know that insane old guy in Patchogue, the one that drives around in that bus, like *all* the time?"

"Ewww, Patchogue," someone says.

"That's Stone's Dad."

"You're kidding."

"I guess something awful happened to him during Helga. Stone never talks about it."

"But he's not dead?"

"No."

"I don't think you can say that you've lost someone if they're still alive."

"You are more than welcome to take that up with Stone when he returns."

"No thanks," concludes the intern, clearly a bit uncomfortable in the pressure-packed environment.

3

The big bad sky is the color of arrogant disinterest. It's looming, just posing there ready to hurl, but forces you to wait, wary. Patchogue: Marco Salazar hates that word, all huge and white on the ugly green road sign. Patchogue: it sounds like a poisonous radish or a burrowing rodent that should have fur but doesn't. It's impossible to say it without spraying it. Patchogue: the only word his mother *could* pronounce—everyone else drooled when they said it.

This debonair gentleman, this *Salazar*, shifts his black wide-tired ride into third gear, just cruising down the Long Island Expressway. He's rocking out, thinking of his old pal Stone as he ashes his cigarette out the window so elegantly you'd think everyone was watching. He likes to smoke in his car. He likes to pump the volume and ride on people's bumpers in a threatening auto ass-rape fashion— he gets off on the fear in their rearview. But really, they're just annoyed and cold, and the coffee mug in their cupholder is not filled with spicy seasonal spacebrew, and their jobs don't pay seven or eight figures, and there is no opportunity for upward mobility, and their lunch often comes wrapped in plastic, and they're not fucking their non-existent assistant, and they'd seriously prefer to avoid confrontation during another mundane morning commute. When they stare helplessly at Marco through the rearview he smiles at them, cigarette between his teeth like a delighted pirate.

Salazar is on his way to the Egostatistical headquarters in Jersey City, NJ. Mostly all of his employees are already on-site and have commenced with morning caffeine rituals. They're frenetic and their speech is physical—a mid to high level joke can arouse near hysteria. They gesticulate from their arms and move their hips all around, bending up and down and really annunciating and accentuating certain words—cursing is cool, well-behaved doggies get down, in just two years employees have worn a path from the open office seating section to the kitchen that houses three, that's right, *three* Jura one-touch espresso makers. Take a sweet pull with your nostrils, rookie, you can smell the rich grounds from there. One can identify new employees by their frothy milk mustaches, presets for cappuccino and macchiato must be known because the labels are worn away—this shit is café-quality.

"Where's Marco," chirps the office weasel. "Where's the boss," he adds, looking around, pulling at his always too tight shirt collar. He stretches and recoils his neck so routinely it makes those around him uncomfortable. His face is squirrelly looking and so thin it seems to have spent time inside a vise. His eyes are grotesquely beady, like two black olives staring out through miniscule peepholes, and he's not even squinting—his mere presence suggests that his only talent may be interviewing for a job.

"He's probably on his way, George," replies Lana.

"*Oh*," he stretches, "how'd *you* know?"

Lana ignores him. She's already self-started boxing up pictures of Marco and Melanie (that's the ex-fiancé).

"Boss better watch it today, those bastards down there look like they could kill."

"He'll be fine, George. I'm sure he appreciates your concern."

The bastards the weasel refers to here have become known as The Number 2s, or just the 2s. This is a protest group of largely Hispanic receptionists and telephone operators replaced or displaced by Marco Salazar's Automated Answering Service—the invention on which Egostatistical Corp. is founded. The thing is, Marco Salazar originally had a partner whom he forgot to give credit to, *or even thank*, after receiving the prestigious award for most significant technological development (STD) of the new millennium. This other dude, LaMichael Carmichael (patent editor and cofounder) became incensed by the omission. He'd put his life on the line for the company, and he was sick of it, sick of Marco, of Marco's fucking face in *all* the magazines: *WIRED*, *PC Magazine*, *Discover*, *Gizmag*, etc, the speech was the last straw—and so Carmichael phoned the editor over at *High-Tech Times*.

The headline of the Carmichael interview read, "The Real Inventor of The Automated Answering Service?" and in the text below a few wretched details did come to light: Carmichael alleged that Salazar had made lucrative agreements with several cellphone service providers in which he promised to program the AAS to ask meaningless and unanswerable questions like "What is your account number?" This is true. Carmichael also claimed that Salazar developed a second generation AAS behind his back that guaranteed callers would be kept on hold for hours while non-existent operators were supposedly busy with other non-existent customers. LaMichael said companies that installed the second-generation software were given a kickback by cellphone service providers and that a percentage of this kickback went to Marco Salazar. This is unconfirmed.

But the most troubling allegation of all dealt with the option to press two for Español—something Marco Salazar had never considered. Paragraphs upon paragraphs of the *Times* article discussed, in graphic detail, the patent editor's daily need to remind Salazar to include an option for the Spanish-speaking public. "It was like he didn't care about them at all," Carmichael concluded.

At first, no one cared about Carmichael's boring interview. But then one day a large group of recently unemployed Hispanic citizens gathered in the Egostatistical parking lot with a brand and a purpose and a lot of free time. They pushed protest signs into the air that called Marco Salazar a racist sonofabitch. Street-level insiders whispered that LaMichael Carmichael was behind the whole thing, or at least came up with the idea to call them The Number 2s—though he receives no credit from the 2s. *High-Tech* sent a reporter to the scene to collect some colorful quotations from the protestors.

The reporter collected one from Daniela, who, while wearing a conservative navy blue business suit was met by her employer after returning from lunch, on a Friday, and told that they'd just installed the Automated Answering Service and that the company wouldn't need her services anymore. Daniela pleaded—she had a mother in hospice care and a daughter just starting kindergarten and a deadbeat husband. "He sends us pizzas out here like that's gonna pay my bills," Daniela said of Marco through interpreter and fellow protestor Juan Miguel, who tucked his blue button front shirt into his khakis for work on a Friday but never even made it to the lobby elevator. "I'm sorry Juan Miguel," his boss told him, "but we've just installed the Automated Answering Service." The bilingual Juan resisted, "Surely, you'll still need someone to deal with the Spanish-speaking customers?" "No Juan Miguel," his boss replied, "there's an option for that." And after twenty-five years of non-essential employment Juan Miguel was terminated and given nothing but ninety-eight weeks of unemployment. "He drives in here everyday smoking and smiling at us—Mr. Carmichael was right, he doesn't care about anyone but himself."

Yes, sad stories across the board, yet still no one really noticed. Finally the reporter saddled up alongside the wide-tired ride for a reactionary quote from the man himself. "Mr. Salazar?" the diminutive reporter asked from behind his spectacles. "Yeah?" Marco replied, stomping out his cigarette on the way in. "What do you think of automation and how many jobs it's costing? What do *you* think of The Number 2s?" Admittedly, not really thinking of The Number 2s, Marco replied, "I don't give a shit." The statement became an instant insensitivity classic, a corny fecal faux pas splattered directly into the many pained faces—confirmation of patent racism. It didn't take long for the whole mess to spread around the capital 'I' Internet. Do I need to explain what clever Internet individuals do with a story involving one hot, young, fabulously wealthy software entrepreneur, one minority group, and a few juicy out-of-context quotations?

They invent clever captions for unrelated pictures.

They use this symbol (#) to reinforce everything already overtly hilarious about the caption's relationship to the unrelated photos.

They look up the word 'injustice' in the dictionary.

They mount high horses.

They form sentences that involve phrases like 'this country' or 'the government.'

They influence late night television monologues.

They want to join the conversation.

They want to join the movement.

They want to do *something* about *it*.

They want Marco Salazar to apologize publicly for what he did.

Another public figure commits a newer and/or funnier faux pas.

They move on.

They leave The Number 2s behind.

And while most of the general public has moved off the story the 2s remain in the Egostatistical parking lot, in the cold, jerking their signs up and down and jeering loudly for Boss Salazar's notice. He steps out of the car and they yell, "BOOOOOOOOOOOO" at him. The signs are in Spanish so Salazar cannot read them but he can see the number 2 featured prominently and also, of course, the word "dos." Some signs show unflattering depictions of the software man with a pencil thin mustache and devil horns. They yell at him en Español throughout his short walk to the door—it's no bother because Marco, naturally, has the closest parking space that isn't handicapped reserved.

In the elevator Boss Salazar stares up at the mirrored ceiling and reconfigures the front of his hairdo, just so— yeah that's good. He pulls a cellular device from his jacket pocket and uses the small, mirrored portion on the back to closely inspect his nostrils for boogers. In the winter months Marco lacks the flexibility required to use the mirrored ceiling for nostril inspection. It's important to him, and most other bosses, to stay booger-free because those nasty specks can really undermine one's authority in the workplace—tiny food particles flying from the boss's mouth or sticking to his or her lips have this same effect. You probably never think about it and that's because the boss is always thinking about it.

The entire executive office turns as the elevator doors open to reveal Marco Salazar in his black leather jacket.

"Is that the boss?" the weasel giggles excitedly, pulling at his collar with two fingers as he stretches his neck out. "Boss coming in now..."

They stand up and cheer when Boss Salazar rolls in. Today is a big day—word has come down that yesterday legal officially quelled The Número Uno Rebellion once and for all. You see, old Juan Miguel out there, he's much more than a sign holding protestor. His kid is a decently hot, somewhat young, Hispanic software engineer. After the branding of the 2s he worked with his father (and possibly...LaMichael Carmichael) on an Automated Answering Service that allowed Hispanic callers to press "1" or "número uno" for Español. For months the 2s spent their time phoning local establishments to see who still used the outdated, or "dos" system, then they'd picket and protest accordingly. The honor of being number one, especially set against Marco's unfortunate reminder of what the number two has been associated with in the past, provided the needed momentum for Juan Miguel Junior's system to cut heavily into Egostatistical profits— something needed to be done. A buyout... "Throw a little cash their way," the legal department said. "Offer Junior a VP spot, put some shine on it." J.M. Jr., honoring his father's wishes, did not accept the position.

While Marco still refuses to make uno the option for Español, he is now the only one with the right to do so, should he ever decide to. The point, in *all* cases, is that number one is reserved for the most popular selection: at a bank one is pay your bills, at the movies one is for show times, at a hidden jungle sex safari one is for directions.

"Okay, okay," the boss waves his thanks.

The weasel cranes his neck toward the boss (he's had too many espressos), "We're finally number one, *and* two!" George rejoices, people kind of laugh, but look sideways at one another. It's clear that George thought of the line weeks ago—he always does that.

"Way to go, Marco," they yell, clapping and whooping and laughing so delightedly that you'd think there was a looming pizza party.

Lana comes out of Marco's office to greet him. She's holding a box and the boss knows what's inside it. Lana looks incredible for someone who didn't shower before work. The boss is getting a little emotional about her appearance when the weasel's stupid voice cracks into his ear. This voice, Marco has said, is to the ears what straight vinegar is to the tongue.

"Heyyya, *Marco*, yo, *BOSS*-man," George says.

Lana notices her employer's eyes clasp shut and his cheeks pinch together.

"Yeah?" Marco replies. He does not know the weasel's

name—Lana estimates Marco only knows, for certain, two or three names in the entire office. The boss is busy and some perplexing department called Human Resources does all the hiring these days anyway. Whenever George speaks, Salazar curses the strange department and wonders where the fuck it came from—his company is in fact the producer of inhuman resources. George always drinks too many espressos and babbles aimlessly. National catastrophes seem to set him off and require more espresso, more neck stretching and collar pulling. Anything that provides for opinionated conversation, like an airport shooting or natural disaster, and stories that involve weather that could possibly lead to a day off send him into frenzy. Whenever the weasel gets yapping, Marco thinks further about Human Resources, and inhuman resources—'maybe it's *non*-human,' he considers, before debating what Alien Resources might entail—a directory of available extra terrestrials?

"So whaddaya think?" George asks.

Lana, being detail oriented, has noticed that Marco wasn't paying attention to George's riff on the allegedly impending Glaze Event. She uses her outstanding verbal communication skills to let George know, "We'll see what happens tomorrow, for now plan on being here."

"But that weatherman seemed scared, didn't he?" George continued. "He's never like that, I've *never* seen him like *that* before..." With each accent the neck cranes out, "Boss, you ever hear about a Glaze Event before?"

"Not before this morning." The boss cracks a smile at his executive assistant.

"You have a call in five minutes, Marco," Lana says.

"Was that supposed to be like a hilarious pun or something?" Lana says, now inside Marco's cozy and carpeted twenty-fourth floor office.

"What?" Marco asks.

"The Glaze Event...this *morning*." She's waving her hands around to suggest that Marco is acting like a clown.

"There was no pun intended, just a comment on the weather report."

"I think people should own their puns if they make them, Marco."

"Do I have a call or what?"

"It's not until this afternoon. I just figured you wanted to get out of that conversation with George."

"*Ah*, yeah, *George*. Almost went with Greg... What's he do, anyway?" Marco asks.

"George is a field tech."

"Go on."

"He goes out to offices and fixes glitches."

"Don't most offices have their own IT professionals?"

"Yup."

"Does our software ever really get messed up?"

"Nope."

"I didn't think so," the boss says, proudly. "So that's why he's here all the time."

"You got it."

"Can we get him his own off—"

"Already tried it..."

"You're such a self-starter."

She smiles.

"What happened?"

"He came out all the time. And he had an ego about it."

"Jesus."

"I know."

"Okay, then fire him. I can't take it. He drives people nuts with that neck thing."

"We can't fire him."

"Why?"

"Because George is Hispanic, Marco."

"*George* is Hispanic?"

"His real name is Jorge."

"Jesus *fuck*—I'm gonna deal with this forever. I forget one fucking thing...I'm the least racist person in the world. Who *is* even racist anymore?"

"People in the south are, I think."

"See, *that's* racist," the boss says.

"You should just tell people what happened, tell them what was going on while you were doing the work—they'll understand."

"Not happening. Listen, should we have a party tomorrow? Celebrate the buyout?"

"You're the boss."

"Send out an email to everyone—we'll have it at my place. We've been in this office too much lately."

"At your *house*, Marco?"

"Yeah... Should be good, right?"

"I'm not coming until those pictures are gone."

"Tell everyone to come at eight."

"Take down those pictures."

"And don't invite George, okay?"

"You sure?"

"Yes, he gets on everyone's nerves—I think we all need to blow off a little steam. Listen to them out there, it's crazy."

"They've just had too much caffeine. I told you not to get *three* machines."

"Do you want one?"

"Yeah..."

"Take one with you today then, that's fine."

"I really think you should invite George to the party."

"Not happening."

For the rest of the day George circles the office, moving from desk to desk, weaseling about the possibility of a Glaze Event—the chance for a day off. He rattles on about a stat he just looked up that states ice glazing can increase tree branch weight by up to one hundred X.

"Whole trees could fall over," he exclaims, and receives disappointing and unenthusiastic replies no greater than: wow, crazy, sounds bad, terrible, boy, man, god, shit, fuck, uh oh, oh my, oh jesus and balls. George returns to his desk to do a bit more research. He pinches the handle of his espresso cup between his thumb and fingers. The cup rattles on its saucer. The light from the computer screen barely penetrates his irides. "Cascade failure," he says so quietly to himself, "oh *my*."

He gets up and fills his espresso and tries this new nugget on for size. "Hey Linda, hey Luke, hey Leah and Shawn..." they're all looking at Shawn's screen, "...what's that—what are you looking at?"

"*Nothing*, George," Shawn replies. The rest of the crew disperses to make it seem like they were also looking at nothing.

"Is that a group email?" the weasel asks.

"No," Shawn says.

"I didn't get one..."

"It's not an email, George," Shawn says.

The weasel puts his cup down, saucer-less, on Shawn's desk—something Shawn repeatedly tells George he does not like.

"Cascade Failure," George says, out of context, looking directly at Shawn's face.

"What?" Shawn asks with a burst of laughter.

"What do you think of it?"

"I have no fucking clue what you're talking about, man."

"I'm talking about Cascade *fucking* Failure, Shawn—count on it."

"What *is* it?"

"Oh, well, it's only a domino effect of falling power lines brought on by a Glaze Event."

"Oh, jeez, that sounds dangerous."

"It is dangerous—actually, it can be devastating."

The weasel stretches his neck. Linda, Luke, and Leah are now gathered in front of the screen on Leah's desk. George is getting anxious, sweat on his brow—he decides to aggressively tuck his brick button front shirt deep into his khakis and make a loud attention-seeking sigh.

"What's going on?" he whispers to himself. George

refills his espresso and knocks on Marco's door.

"Yo, *BOSS*-man?"

"Yes, George," Marco says.

"Did you get a group email? Did Lana send out an office email today, like, just now maybe?" He pulls his collar.

"Not that I know of, George. I don't get the group emails anyway."

The weasel goes back to his desk and refreshes his office email three times, sips his espresso, refreshes again: nothing.

4

She laid the lump of calf muscle on the edge of an ottoman. Her son sat on this orange ottoman and accepted the calf in his hands, her bruised and useless foot met with his crotch.

"Dunnever furget hooyarrr," Claudia Salaznek said, drooling a bit.

"No, Mom," Mark replied. He gripped the limp calf with his fingertips and massaged it just like the doc had shown him. Dr. Engelberger had demonstrated the proper technique by gently kneading a water balloon, and that's what the calf felt like—a bulbous, juicy, pale mass of loose filament, dangling and worthless, more sideshow or prank than something of matter in the world. After three minutes of pulsing Mark performed the squeeze and release, in which he took the entire calf in his palms, like sizing up an eggplant, and gripped it tightly, then let go all at once. Upon release the calf would flop, wobble and hang.

Mark's mother sat on the couch, smoking. Her right hand waved back and forth from the right side of her mouth to an end table ashtray. She cashed the smoke from her lungs straight into her son's face. He'd developed a taste for it and could distinguish Parliament brand from Marlboro. During the daily massages he'd send his mind away from the immediate scene to contemplate things like the possibility that the corner store clerk couldn't tell if his Mother said "Marlboro" or "Parliament", though Mark knew she preferred Marlboro. Claudia had stopped bothering with small things. And the way words leaked out the corner of her mouth made annunciation impossible— her entire left side unfurling, dead nerves conceding easily to gravity, signified by the trail of saliva that flowed like a river from her sulking lips to her cheek and down along the chin to the neck before collecting on the damp shirt collar. Her whole western hemisphere unraveled bit by bit and delineated a perfect history of deterioration.

Dick Salaznek, worldly philosopher and trainman, sensed something amiss when he came home from work that fall day. The beginning of this little history—chainsaw sprawled out sideways, wires split in half that lay across the lawn willy-nilly, a three-stack of firewood that had never made it to the porch, a bigger stack of firewood on the porch that had never made it inside, and no one inside.

"*Something* is amiss," Dick said to himself, making a cocktail.

Mark returned home late that night, motherless, to find his dad slumped on the couch surrounded by forty or fifty foam pellets.

"Dad," Mark said.

Dick huffed and burped and roused, "Marky?" The living room light stung Dick's eyes. "Where's your mother?"

Mark told him the whole story—the neighbors, the wood, the watches, the chainsaw and the wires.

"I always said she was a real live wire," Dick said, and then got up and went to bed without further comment.

Two days later when Claudia Salaznek cane-bobbed into the house, leaning left like that strange Italian structure, Mark got a real clear read about the future of their family from his father's face. It slacked grotesquely—a mocking mirror of Dick's first glimpse of his altered wife. Claudia still had her humor, mumbling, "Hunny, I'mmome," and went in for a hug, cane and all. Dick did hug her, but you could tell he didn't like it. He didn't squeeze or smile or say 'Oh, thank *God* you're all right.' He opted instead for the negative cliché of drinking and self-loathing. After a few weeks he had to switch couch cushions because he ran out of foam to pick. Claudia sat on that foamless cushion without complaint as her son massaged her leg, hoping to inspire unlikely nerve regeneration. Mark hated the way the cushion's once happy foam face now took the form of a toothless frowning geezer.

Dick and Mark quickly gave up asking Claudia to cane-bob her way outside to smoke cigarettes. It seemed cruel. The motion appeared to be such a painful effort. So the house became rank with ash and dust and cat droppings and dirty old highballs lying around, some with ash and some with unfinished whiskey. After two falls down the stairs, Mark wheeled a cot into the living room to save his Mother the trouble of going upstairs to her bedroom. He placed a bedpan on the living room floor for overnight emergencies.

Teachers whispered about the greasiness of Claudia Salaznek's son's hair and wondered why she was *still* on disability—nobody liked the sub they got for the special needs kids. He didn't give a shit about them. Someone said they heard him use the word "retard". Claudia's friends at the school would corner Mark in the hallway, "How's your mother?" And he'd give nothing away, "Getting better." Mark went straight home everyday after school to massage and feed his mom. He helped her in and out of the tub—he shaved the dead leg. And he sensed Dick's days in the Salaznek house coming to an end.

When Dick got back from punching train tickets he'd look at them and recycle his favorite line, "There she is, my little live wire." He'd head directly into the kitchen for a drink and return with a just-microwaved plastic tray in his other hand. "I'm a *hungry* man," he'd say and slurp from his glass.

"This is the brand new Hungry-Man dinner, Marky. Hungry-Man *Selects*—slow-cooked pulled pork. Ya like one?"

"No thanks."

"C'mon son, look at this sweet corn and potatoes."

"I'm okay."

"What about my apple crumb dessert? I'm not gonna eat it."

"I'm fine."

Dick alternately chewed his Hungry-Man *Selects* and looked at the familiar scene to his left. Chewing, looking, chewing, looking, shaking his head, huffing breath, shows of annoyance.

"Christ Marky, how long you gonna sit there massaging her like that?"

"Another five minutes or so."

Claudia blew cigarette smoke in the direction of the Hungry-Man *Selects* tray.

"No, I mean how *long*?"

"Doctor Engelberger said it could take years."

"*Years*? Furchrissake," Dick said, "it's never gonna work."

"It might." Mark leaned over, and though his Mom sat directly in front of him, whispered, "It's not gonna do her any good to be so negative."

"Well," Dick said, wiping some Hungry-Man from his mouth, "what the *fuck* are you gonna do about her face?"

"WADDABOUTMAHFASCHE?" Claudia jumped in.

Dick took another bite of Hungry-Man. He couldn't look at her to respond. Mark still had his mother's calf in his palms.

"WADDABOUT...MAH...*FUGGIN*-FASCHE?" she asked again.

"Nothing," Dick said, "Nevermind."

Claudia continued to stare at her husband. He was to her right so he could only see her good side. She blew a hit of Marlboro directly into his face. Mark saw that his father's eyes were beginning to well up as he cut at a piece of Hungry-Man meat with white plastic utensils. He took another slug from his glass, swirled the ice around, and said, "I don't know how much longer I can do this," to no one in particular and received no reply. Sounds of Dick's smacking lips and Claudia's wobbly calf filled the room with incredible consistency, chopping back and forth like windshield wipers. The right side of Claudia's face grinned at her next drag. She turned to her husband and covered him in a sheet of Marlboro wind. This called even more attention to the silence. Dick shook his head no. Claudia observed him a second longer as the smoke-cloud lingered. A few kernels of sweet corn slipped from Dick's fork and landed on his Long Island Railroad-man uniform. He left the yellow pebbles there. Claudia took another hit, contemplated it with her lungs, and sent it Dick's way. This massive hit forced Dick to cough a few more kernels from his mouth onto his uniform, which made Mark giggle despite his best efforts to hold back. Mark's laughter inspired his mother's own cackle—everyone's first real laughter since the accident. Everyone except for Dick. Dick is not laughing. Dick is crying. And he's crying in that very shitty way where he thinks no one can tell and he's still trying to eat but his eyes are all red and watery and anyone with decent sight can see his jaw quivering terribly between bites. The extreme mental and physical exertion of an adult male desperately holding back tears hung thick over the toxic atmosphere. Dick stared at his pathetic plastic plate. "You think that's funny," he mumbled through his lips, sadly.

Some of the Salaznek cats took a purring interest in the scene. Claudia sensed her growing audience. She sensed increased anticipation as she pulled another dramatic drag off the Marlboro. Dick turned to his wife, chewing, jaw-trembling; he wanted her to look at him, and she did. Their eyes locked like young lovers. But instead of moving in for a kiss, Claudia's mouth opened and enshrouded her husband's face in a dragon's breath of Marlboro.

Mark stopped giggling then and the kitties quit purring, though both parties remained interested. The lovers' eyes stayed locked until all the smoke cleared. Dick started laughing. Not that joyous cackle, something more maniacal. He placed the plastic knife and fork back onto the half-eaten Hungry-Man *Selects* tray before slamming it into his wife's face—like their wedding cake of yore. He held it against her face and rubbed it in too. Claudia yelled something from behind the tray that sounded like, "YARYARYARRR," her right arm flailed wildly for the tray—her left arm stayed in place. Mark dropped Claudia's leg and jumped to her rescue but the teenager had no chance against the stronger railroad man who threw him on top of his mother. As Dick stood up the yellow sweet corn kernels popped onto the ground and the hungry kitties swarmed. While they were surely delighted by the corn treat, they did also devour a greater amount of the indistinguishable foam pellets. Once the wise cats realized they were ingesting *only* foam, they hopped onto Claudia's lap and moved to her head and face, hoping to get some of the pulled pork now available for public consumption. Claudia tried to push them from her head. "GEDAFUG OFFAMEE," she yelled, kicking her right heel in the air and waving her cane like an angry wizard. Mark dodged the cane, grabbed two of the cats in his arms and tossed them outside. When he came back for the third cat he scooped a generous helping of pulled pork from his mother's hair and threw that outside along with the third cat to keep them all happy.

Claudia grabbed her smoking Marlboro from the ashtray and took a drag. By now Mark had returned from the kitchen with a wet rag. He wiped the pulled pork from his mom's hair, face, shirt. He found Claudia's calm demeanor surprising. They heard Dick zipping bags upstairs.

"Fuggem, Marky," she told her son. "Dunnever furget hoo-yarr boy, ya hear me?"

"Sure Mom, I won't," Mark replied.

Dick dashed out the front door like a real pussy, without a word to either of them.

"Fuggem, Marky, jus' fuggem," Claudia said. "Les go taiggabaf."

"You finish your smoke. I'll run it."

Mark went upstairs and put his hand under the water, waiting for it to warm to his mother's preference—not too hot, but hot enough. He held Claudia's left hand as the two squeezed up the staircase. She used her right to cane-bob one step at a time. It was a tricky operation, they used to end up with four feet per step, but eventually Mark decided to leave one foot behind to brace in case of a fall. In the tub she told him, "Yuhknow wha?"

"What Mom?"

"Maleggs stardin' tafeel a lah betterrr."

"Really?"

"I'm gonta work tomarahh."

"Are you sure?"

"Ya... Daysezz I cancombag wheneverrr I-wan."

The next morning Mark Salaznek woke up to the sounds of cane-bobbing and coffee gurgling—sunrise aboard a pirate ship, me mateys. A pungent waft of thick Canadian bacon climbed the stairwell and inspired feelings of hope.

"MARGYYY COMON MARGY, ISS BREKISTTIME," Claudia yelled, her cane pecking back and forth from stove to table.

"I'm feelin' guuud," she said, sliding a plate in front of Mark.

"That's great, Mom. This looks great too. Especially for a one-handed chef," Mark joked. She tapped him on the head with her cane gently enough to be considered a sign of endearment, "Mahleff side stillwerrrks guudinuf."

And so they chewed, genuinely enjoying their first Dick-free breakfast. A winter frost put a cool squeeze on the sunlight that filled the kitchen and revealed dueling steam pirouettes over Salaznek coffee mugs. Dead tree limbs played peek-a-boo outside the window over the sink. The piercing sigh of school bus air brakes reminded Claudia to ask, "Zit weerrrd if I take dabus taskool?"

"No Mom, it's fine...until you can drive again."

"Zit Boyle?"

"Yeah, Mr. DeFoné is our driver—real good guy, little weird."

"I herdee jus' drivezzda bussall night?"

"I don't know about any of that stuff, Mom."

"Sucha gud boy, mah Margy." She messed his hair.

When the bus arrived to pick up The Salaznek's a bunch of teen punks had their faces pressed against the windows like they were in quarantine—so stupidly close that their unbrushed breath showed on the glass. Claudia went first and Mark behind her in the familiar alignment. The word "cane" shot like a game of lightning telephone from the front to the back of the bus. When Claudia reached the top of the steps, every single student looked directly at her face for two seconds too long. They could see the way the left side looked melted, and it made them laugh. Mark could hear them from the bus's stairwell. His insides started to spiral out of control as he wasn't prepared for this level of embarrassment. He hadn't considered it; this was his mother, and he'd gotten used to her this way. The laughter reminded him of the initial reveal. Doctor Engelberger had told him, "Son, your mother looks, a little...*odd* now, okay? I just want you to be prepared for that—try not to make a face at her." While Mark did do well at not making a face, the same cannot be said for his peers. It was as if a demonic telepathic rhythm poisoned them all—Mark saw fifteen left-eye-winking idiots, shit-stained Cyclopses, and another group of twenty that took to depicting his mother's mouth by fish hooking themselves and drooling and audibly gurgling "Uhhhgggg," so loudly that Boyle DeFoné had to call for silence. This plea made them quit the physical gestures but did induce a good deal of not-so-hushed laughter. Sitting behind his dad, and across the aisle from Mark and Claudia, the hotheaded Stone DeFoné stood up and yelled, "*FUCK* you! Shut the *fuck* up and just leave 'em alone," then sat down. But stood back up and quickly added, "*Fuck* all of you!" for good measure.

"Stone, that's *enough*," Boyle called over his shoulder as he shifted the yellow hellbox into gear. A low hum, bloody murmuring, bubbled up increasingly from the bus's bowels like a pot getting ready to boil. The unpleasant murmuring gave way to the chant of many teenage Indian chiefs HIYAHOWA-HIYAHOWAing with their palms over their mouths as Boyle rolled toward the Weekapaug Middle School speed bump complex—oh, all this Patchogueing and Weekapauging, something to do with the area's once great Native American population—towns named to honor the Indian tribes they displaced. The children were enlightened in Elementary school. You know, the Indians and Pilgrims (certainly a pleasant-sounding name for any group) had a nice meal, talked it over, and decided a few casinos would do the trick—an odd story to maintain in the face of unprecedented modern murdering. Anyway, all that they retained of their Native American education was the chanting speed bump chair jump. As they yell "HIYA-HOWA" they bounce their butts up and down and up and down on that gross plastic bench seating. The dream, the ideal bounce, occurs when the wheel nearest your seat goes over the speed bump just as your butt goes back in the air—with this combination it is possible to bang one's head on the ceiling. The noise of this collision attracts massive attention, applause and laughter from those jealous onlookers who didn't nail the timing. There is nothing any adult can do to combat the bopping as all the children are involved and the one adult is of course driving the bus. One day, some of these children will grow up to teach the same story about Turkey and Casinos to future students who will retain nothing but will inherit the land and this other boneheaded Patchogue tradition of bouncing like a gang of whack-a-moles. It'd be pleasing to think of Claudia Salaznek treating them as such, whacking her cane on their mole heads, but lo, she's too weak.

"Claudia?" one of the hall monitors asked.

Claudia nodded, "Iznit ahvius?"

A flood of screaming kids burst through the doors behind her. They pushed the cane lady out of the way—it's almost time for Christmas break, bitch. Knapsacks bounce off their backs like jockeys on thoroughbreds, their sneakers squeak across the slick and crowded entryway. Their voices are sharp, prepubescent and nonsensical.

"Do you want me to take you to Principal Moran's office, Claudia?" the hall monitor asked.

Claudia nodded again.

Moran gets to school an hour before anyone else. He waves to the morning janitor, "'ello there Billy" on the way to his office where he immediately starts slurping coffee. He'll have to discipline some kids for tardiness this morning, that's for sure. He'll once again define the word truancy for a young boy or girl. There is a meeting today about the possibility of outlawing tank tops this summer (for boys, girls, both?). Should the school continue to fund the local cub scouts troop in the face of diminishing interest? Should...Taco Tuesday...be eliminated? It *is* unhealthy, *yet* delicious, but causing some bad bathroom accidents that Billy has brought up the last three Wednesdays. Why is it that, generally speaking, a principal's appearance often suggests child abuser? They're second only to priests, and if they're both in street clothes, at the diner, you'd never tell one from the other. Moran himself does even look like The Penguin from *Batman*, though taller, and without the comically extended nose. Moran's nose is flatter and round, and if it was stuck instead to his foot might be called a bunion. From what Claudia Salaznek can tell, this guy spends most of his time sifting through file cabinets.

"*Oh...Claudia*," Moran said, stunned, looking over his shoulder with his hands on a file.

"Yar der Morrron," Claudia greeted him.

Moran shut the file cabinet, without taking a file, and waved Mrs. Salaznek into his office. "Do you need help?" he asked as she sat perfectly on one of his big round leather office chairs. There's a bunch of stupid shit on Moran's white office walls. One, a poster that says "Perseverance," in huge letters and depicts a group of soldiers conquering a foreign land—the depiction does not appear to be actual wartime photography but maybe something recreated on a set. The soldiers all look similar, handsome, but none handsome enough to be a model. Bachelor of Arts Degree: SUNY Brockport. Masters Degree: SUNY Buffalo. There is a dying plant hanging from the ceiling behind Moran's left shoulder—his office is windowless. His bookshelf is turned so guests cannot see the titles, and a bowl of plastic fruit rests oddly between Moran and his Special Needs Director.

"So, Claudia, how are you feeling?" he asks, slurps his mug—his bald head shines beneath the humming and cruel fluorescent lighting.

"I'm doin'alaht betterrr axeshully."

"Well...Claudia," slurp, "I gotta tell ya, we were just thinking—"

"Yar?"

"We were thinking that being *on site*," he puts his fingers up as quotations, "might not be the most productive use of your time anymore."

"Ahnsite? Yoojus' mean hereacht da school?"

"That's right. Your being here, *on site*—it might not be

what's best for the children."

Claudia's left shoulder slumps down a bit and her right leg kicks out against Principal Moran's desk.

"Waddamah suppos tado?"

"You can consult with the new Special Needs Director—I've cleared some room in the budget, a modest salary—and of course you'll still get your disability. So that should do it."

"I wanna teesh," Claudia said.

"Miss Salaznek..." he slurps, "*I'm* having a difficult time understanding you now. How do you think your students, who already have comprehension issues, will respond? It's also, it's, well, goll-ee Claudia, how can I say this..." he's touching his sweaty bald head; when he does it you can see caked-in yellow stains in his pits.

"Juzzay it."

"Putting you in front of those kids, it's kind of like a cruel *mirror* at this point—if you know what I mean."

"Bahhhhh," Claudia replied harshly and stood up. "Tahell with ya, ta *hell*!" She pointed her cane definitively in Moran's face and left.

"Mrs. Salaznek, where are you going?" asked the hall monitor, but it was too late. Claudia Salaznek was out the door and on her way to buy some cigarettes.

"Fuggem," she said to herself, bobbing down the road. "Furgetaboudat shhhit."

She walked into a corner store, still five blocks from her house: "Packamahrbros." The cash register artist handed her Parliaments. "Ten bucks," he said.

"Yar, tenbux furda wrong fuggin brandasmokes."

The cash register artist smiled and took her twenty—handed back ten dollars.

Claudia moved on down the block, kerplunk-kerplunk-kerplunk, large cloudpuffs ballooning overhead at precise intervals, like a steamship leaving port. Boyle's school bus circled a two-block perimeter around Claudia's position—she heard the shrill air brakes at every intersection. She longed for that bus but was sadly surrounded by a gang of one-ways. The bus passed in front of her and Boyle snapped his head her way. He knew her by the cane but couldn't turn down that street. He took a left and another left but blew by the street in his excitement. "Ah Jeez-*us*, missed her again." He smacked the giant steering wheel. Hit the intersection, air brakes, left, left, another look: cane still in place though Claudia has bobbed quite a ways since the last time he circled the block. Three more lefts before arrival: "Goin' somewhere?" Boyle DeFoné unfolded his doors.

"Yar," Claudia replied. Two attached stop signs unfurled their universal red message. Claudia took so long to get up the stairs that three cars piled up behind the bus and some asshole actually felt justified blowing his horn. He said, "Come on," but you couldn't hear it because his windows were up.

Claudia sat in Stone's seat directly behind Boyle. She rested the entire left side of her body against the cold glass. Boyle didn't say a word, just drove her home.

"Thang-ya Buuyull," Claudia said, going down the steps. She walked in front of the bus, into the driver's field of vision and waited like a good girl. Boyle checked the rearview, stop signs flashed in the quiet street, then he waved Claudia across. And although Boyle DeFoné is a bit dimwitted, it doesn't take a genius to appreciate the amount of effort and courage necessary for Claudia to cross the street. As he watched her he had time to wonder why the little deformed lady wore such heavy boots, and why she didn't have a hat on, and how does anyone's hair become so dry, and why the hell isn't her husband driving her around? She turned and waved to Boyle after she'd made it across the street. He waved back and commenced circling the neighborhood until school let out.

Mrs. Salaznek looked at the empty space where her woodpile used to be and her frown slid south a fraction further. Her Dwarf Alberta Spruce withered in wait of

Santa's restoration. "Fuggem," she said to herself, walked inside, grabbed Dick's old whiskey, poured a tumbler and took a stiff honk of refreshment from the right side of her face, and then poured another.

5

"Yo, that's DeFoné right there dude. Look!"

"Nah, no way. DeFoné doesn't come around here."

Two fellas hang smoking their cigarettes under the neon glow of *Tanked*, the best bar in Patchogue. Stone notices them but keeps it moving.

"Dude, it's him. Look at that fuckin' suit," this one continues. "YO! DUH-FO-NEE?"

Stone turns around, "Yeah?"

They break up laughing. They're rocking brown Carhartt jackets—both of them, and wool ski caps, too. They're also equally chubby and goateed—the bullseye effect created by plugging the smokes into their mouths is unflattering.

"What's up with that weather report this morning?"

"What?" Stone asks, pulling his scarf tight around his neck.

"GLAZED fucking *EVENT*?" they laugh. "Come on, you're jerkin' us, right?" Both men perform the universal motion for jerkin' us.

"It's coming," Stone replies.

"Yeah, I bet it is."

Stone approaches the two men: "Listen, has either of you seen a bus driving around here?"

"What bus? Like, your *dad's* bus?" the one says.

"Good ole bumble bee?" adds the other.

"Yeah, he's around here—he'll be in for his nectar in a few hours."

"You haven't seen him? I can't wait around."

"What, you gotta go do *The Evening News* or some shit," they laugh.

"Yes, actually that is exactly where I have to go."

"Oh," the one says.

"Oh shit," adds the other.

"Right," replies Stone.

"Give it a minute, we heard him buzzing around last time we came out to smoke," says the first guy as he holds his hand in the air, calling for silence. Stone and the other smoker wait for him as one would a prophet on the verge of a transcendent message.

"Ah, *there*," he says, "you hear it?"

Stone is off after the echo of air brakes. Before he leaves he warns the smokers that they'd better gas up their generators tonight.

"Yeah, go fuck yourself weatherman," one says under his breath.

Stone power-walks three blocks, then stops and listens.

PUH-*FOOSH*.

He shoots west three more blocks. A faint odor of diesel lingers in the air.

PUH-*FOOSH*.

There it is—two blocks dead ahead. He can see the taillights flashing at the next intersection. The meteorologist jogs carefully in his brown oxfords that click-click-click-click against the frozen sidewalk, his scarf flapping in the breeze behind him. Stone's arms do pump a pretty wonderful form, damn shame no one is around to appreciate his motion. Just sleepy specialty shops—real estate offices, local lawyers with professional sounding names like Hammerstein, florists, beerists, bagelists, a cute bakery and the like. The ocean swishes in and out a few blocks away and the horizon shoots from the wood-shingled roofs all the way to space.

Stone sees the bus take a left. It's only a block away. He can hear his own breath bounce as he runs—the taste of diesel is getting thick.

He runs alongside the bus: "BOYLE," he yells.

PUH-*FOOSH*. The bus stops.

Stone is on the driver's side of the street so he must walk into the driver's field of vision. The red stop signs unfurl, brighter than usual in the darkening evening. Boyle checks the rearview before waving his son to cross the street.

"Goin' somewhere?" Boyle asks, unfolding the doors.

Stone climbs the three-step well and slumps down, tired from running, in the seat to Boyle's right.

"Where ya headed?" Boyle asks, casually steering the big wheel like a tour guide through a ghost town.

"Dad, it's me—*Stone.*"

"Where ya headed then?" Boyle asks.

"I'm not going anywhere...I came here to talk."

"Gotta be goin' somewhere... Everybody's goin' somewhere."

"Dad, there's another ice storm coming—tomorrow. You need to come and stay at the house."

"Everybody comes from somewhere," Boyle replies, steering.

"You're not listening. It's gonna be worse than *Helga.*"

"Helga's a fucking cunt."

"Dad you can't sleep on the bus, you'll freeze."

"Say, where's your friend Marky?"

"*Jesus* Dad, I don't fucking know. Old Brookville, I think..."

"Haven't seen his sweet mother around town..."

"Dad, listen to me..." Stone reaches out and grabs Boyle's right arm. He pulls it off the wheel and Boyle slams the brakes. PUH-*FOOSH*.

"Look at me," Stone says.

Boyle shifts the bus back into gear and swings a slow right. There's a pedestrian on the corner so he unfolds the doors.

"Goin' somewhere?"

Before the pedestrian can answer Stone stands up and pulls the lever shut. He smacks his Father in the face, his own face is getting red—he's becoming hyper and hot and slightly uncombed. "Listen to me for once in your *fucking* life," he yells.

Boyle shifts the bus into gear and it lurches forward. He takes a left and keeps looking around for anyone who might need a ride.

"If you stay on this bus tonight and tomorrow, you are going to die."

Boyle starts laughing, takes another left, and then says, "Buzzzzz, buzz, buzz, the bumble bee goes buzz, buzz, buzz." He swings his head to the fine rhythm.

"Dad, it's going to be worse than Helga. Do you hear me? Do you remember what happened during Helga?"

"Helga's a fucking cunt," he says, and takes a left.

Stone stuffs a piece of paper into Boyle's shirt pocket. "That's my address, okay?" But Boyle isn't paying attention so Stone grabs his father's chin and turns it, they're only inches apart and Stone's nostrils are flaring heroically, "*Please*," he breathes, "just come to the house—stay as long as you like." Stone releases his dad's face, his tone less than inviting.

Boyle swings another left and arrives once again at the forlorn pedestrian. "Goin' somewhere?" he asks. The pedestrian approaches the three-step stairwell as Stone leaves.

"*Hey*, it's Stone DeFoné," the pedestrian says with Christmas-type cheer.

Stone tries to walk away and remain calm, but the pedestrian yells to him. "What's up with this Glaze Event, guy? You're just jerkin' us, right? Just to be safe?"

Stone turns and walks back to the pedestrian. He pulls him down from the first step and takes him by the coat then shoves him locker-style up against one side of the unfolded plastic doors. "Oh it's *coming*, you stupid motherfucker." Stone's face is red, he's hyper-pissed, the lonely pedestrian doesn't deserve this treatment. "Fill up your generator, stock up on non-perishables, hunker down—it's coming."

6

Back at the offices of Egostatistical Corp. good boss Salazar sips an espresso minimug while listening to the details Re: The Número Uno buyout. Boring. This happens over the speakerphone—business types refer to this situation as a conference call. When these types tell you, or anyone, and likely *everyone*, that they are now on or will soon be on a *conference call* they look at you and then into the sky to show how serious things are now or will be in a moment. Marco estimates the entire conference could have been completed in less than ten minutes, but here they are, forty-five minutes down the road, and every person on the call has yawned at least once, save Marco, who will go out of his way to avoid any semblance of a yawn—he'll even fake cough or sneeze to disguise a yawn.

He is lucky that this isn't an in-person conference because then it would be a full-blown meeting. And then he wouldn't be allowed to pass the time staring at the last unboxed office photo of Melanie. She's so smiley, and they're on a beach, and she'd asked someone to take a photo of them holding each other in front of some blue vacation water—something Marco disliked, bothering unknown others for a snap. But he's glad for it now. Her smile has caused traffic accidents, it makes conference calls bearable, it's big and white and crazy in the world, it loves everything equally, and when combined with her eyes gives the impression of a mothering tigress—nurturer, protector, fluid beauty. The sun hits her shoulders, her brown hair has a silky sheen; it's so soft that Marco thinks she must shower in velvet.

He realizes the photo is a test as he tosses it in the box with the rest. Lana has left just that one pristine picture, because she's clever like that—she wants *him* to box it. She has above average communication skills.

"That all sound good to you, Marco?" the phone cuts in.

"*Perfect*," answers Marco. "You making any progress getting these pieces of shit out of my parking lot?"

"That joke really isn't funny, and it's not *your* parking lot, Marco. We rent it—that's part of the problem."

"What the fuck?"

"Until they make too much noise, or harm someone, or try to enter the building, you're stuck with them—and you can't provoke them, that wouldn't count."

"What about the kids? The little kids—they used to learn to ride bikes and stuff in our lot. They're all gone now."

"It's the dead of winter, Mr. Salazar."

"*Before* that...they scared the kids away this summer."

"We'll look into it."

"Great," Marco says, and pushes the button that ends the conference call.

The weasel is sneaking around outside the boss's office. Rolling yawns pass from cubicle to cubicle like a stadium wave. It's getting to be late afternoon and Jorge is aware that he's more tolerable when people are too tired to be annoyed.

"Ohhhh yaaaawww-humph, what is it George?"

"Leah," he starts, "have you ever heard of Cascade Failure?"

"No, what is it?" She's not looking at him, or listening.

The weasel presents a list of statistics he's just looked up on his computer. He doesn't know what he's saying but he knows Leah's not listening—what he's doing is staring at her computer. He knows everyone in the office keeps their office email up all the time at the end of the day so it always looks like they're up to something important. Leah's not exactly reading an email, per se, but her inbox is on full display, and the weasel locks onto his target: "Celebrating The Número Uno Buyout at Marco's place!" is the subject, and the original sender is Lana Burke.

"...and so like basically with the added weight from all the ice, that's the glazing effect, trees with weak branch junctions have an increased risk for potential damage—*especially* in stronger winds."

"That's really interesting, George. Um, so, I have a conference call in a few minutes that I need to prepare for..." She looks at George, and then at the ceiling.

"Oh, yeah, I see, okay, sure..." George walks away, hoping she hadn't caught him staring at her inbox.

Marco emerges from his office with the cardboard box full of Melanie. Lana stands up and peeks into his office. "Good," she says. Marco considers briefly that she's forgetting who the boss is, but lets it go. "I'm headed out," he informs her mid-stride. Several meager goodbyes rise from the open office seating: "Bye Marco," "Night Boss," "See ya tomorrow Marco." Marco can sense the weasel headed his way but the boss is too smart and too quick— he takes the stairs.

Patpatpatpatpat—patpatpatpatpat, he winds around the hard concrete stairs then exits the building, "BOOOOOOOOOOOOOOOOOOOOOOOOOOOOOOOOOOO OOO,BOOOOOOOOOOOOOOOOOOOOOOOOOOO,"
The 2s pump their protest signs and perk back to life at the sight of him. He knows they leave the lot and take

breaks during the day. He watches from his office window and is aware that, like dogs, they're now onto his schedule.

"What are you still doing out here, Juan Miguel?" Marco asks.

Juan Miguel looks awkwardly about, pulls his winter cap down almost over his eyes and says, "What? Where should I be, mang?"

"Probably home partying with Juan Junior—you're rich now."

Juan Miguel uses his protest sign that reads, "You're the piece of shit," to shield his face from his amigos. "Shut the fuck up, mang," he whispers at Marco and makes that threatening, like, not-in-front-of-my-friends face.

"*¿De qué está hablando Juan?*" one of the other 2s inquires.

"*De nada,*" Juan says.

Marco is merciful. He's established that Juan Miguel should watch his step, but he doesn't want to jeopardize his fresh victory so he lets it go. "I know none of you like me, but I'm telling you, you shouldn't come here tomorrow—there's gonna be a bad storm—you'll get stuck."

"*Está mintiendo.*"

"*No le importamos una mierda.*"

"*Ese hombre del tiempo no tiene ni idea.*"

"We're not going anywhere," Juan Miguel says for the group.

"This won't end well for you, Juan," Marco says.

"We'll jes have to see about that, won't we?" Juan retorts.

"Whatever you say, Juan—tell Junior to give me a ring, all right?"

"Fuck you, mang," Juan says, pumping his sign up and down.

This inspires the jacketed group behind Juan to start jerking their signs and catcalling and booing and whistling again.

"I don't know why he bothers," Lana mumbles from the window.

"Boss is a nice dude," the weasel says. "He never leaves anyone out in the cold." Lana jumps. *Ah.* She hadn't realized the weasel is standing right behind her. She turns around and he's still that close—their toes almost touch. Despite this insane proximity she still can't see into his eyes. George's lips are chapped and browned by his prolific caffeine intake.

"Right?" he asks.

"What?" Lana replies, turning from George's repulsive breath.

"Boss would never leave anyone out in the cold, right?"

"That's right, George."

He stares at her: "You sure?" He tilts his head to one side, no response, tilts it to the other side, examining her, casting the breath to wear down her defenses, and still, nothing. Lana's communication skills far exceed George's, she's easily aware of what he's getting at.

"It's time to go home now, George."

"Ohhhhhh yeahhhhh," Weasel pulls his collar to the side, blasts his neck out opposite, "it's quittin' tiiiiiiiiiiiiiiiiiiiiiiiime."

Marco's already in his ride. He revs it hard then presses the personally designed old-school cigarette car lighter into its socket. Out his left window the 2s protest his choice of automobile—it's showy and fast and sexy and he's correct in assuming that at least some part of them is jealous.

He pulls up to Juan Miguel and rolls down the window—the crowd goes silent in the presence of Marco's car. They can hear the cigarette car lighter pop out on the ready and they whisper to each other about the very cool possibility of Marco Salazar having one of *those* in *that* car.

"Don't come here tomorrow," Marco tells Juan Miguel.

As Juan Miguel starts to speak Marco hammers the accelerator, rolls up the window, and burns away, laughing. He checks the rearview, yes, a bunch of popcorn kernels bouncing and jerking their signs and yelling things he can't hear. He applies the car lighter's coil to his smoke and pulls the delightful mixture into his system. The city buildings recede into the dusty winter sunset and Salazar kicks up the jams—he's a rock enthusiast, he knows lyrics and history, performances and legends, none of those bullshit ballads cemented on radio repeat either—the good shit, the whiskey on the floor dancing in leather boots music—the stuff fills his guts—this is not a man who can tolerate top 40 for more than three seconds though he's becoming familiar with how odd those artists' lives must be. He plays the air guitar when the notion takes him, like now: "Take me back down where the cool water flows *y'allll*—let me remember things I love. Stoppin' at the log where catfish bite, walkin' along the river road at night—barefoot girls dancin' in the moonlight."

"*Shit-chyeahh*," he says.

That last line takes him. He has seen Melanie dancing barefoot many times. There's nothing like it—alone on their home carpet, across the various dance floors at many old friends' weddings, he holds her small shoes until he can't help but join her and even yeah, sure, dear *god* has he seen it on the beach in the moonlight, feet flopping about below her arms that fly haphazardly in the sky. These people who can jam together and dance, they're different from the Top 40 crowd who fuck and fight like bullfrogs waiting to croak in the invisible distance. Marco's struck by this whim of sentimentality and considers the boxed-up remains on the seat next to him the greatest disaster—a cardboard receptacle of remembrances in place of the real thing. He takes out his phone to call her but the song ends. He puts the device back in his pocket: "Stay cool, Marco."

Inside the mansion it's time to pump iron. Marco devours a shake, just like his dietician showed him. "Yeah," he burps, wipes his mouth clean—wipes his wrist on his pants (he's not wearing a shirt). The basement gym is all mirrored and professionally clean. Melanie and Marco used to fuck down here—she kinda liked it when he would get pumped with no shirt on—this was their place for fucking. They'd never make love here. It's impossible to make love in a basement surrounded by metal equipment, Melanie insisted—and correctly so. Things can happen in a basement that should never happen in the Master Suite, as a general rule.

Marco tunes the flat screen televisions to the News and starts in on some serious curls. A new, prettier anchor details the day's chaos wrought by the approaching storm. Eyewitness accounts of road rage turned violent, people taking sides, bread battles in the aisles so severe the last loaf split open and went to the birds. A recurring warning about *not* turning one's thermostat above ninety-five—a related video essay about the dangers of using one's oven to heat the house. A touching story about a local girl who delivered peanut butter and jelly to her disabled neighbor: "I never told her to do it," the girl's mother said, "she just packed up and went right over there. Charity has always been really sweet like that." The anchor muses about all the good in the world.

"What a load of shit," Marco says, "Six...seven...eight, *Charity*..." he grunts, "My ass."

Backstage in the writers' room the atmosphere is dead serious. Stone's hyped. He's on in *ten* (minutes). He's circling the ovular desk where the writing staff and interns sit: "Come on, come on, come *on*...what are we gonna *call* this fucker?"

On a dry erase board are at least eleven names with slashes through them: Mindy, Sherry, Victor, Paula, Patty, Igor, Lee, Rina, Oscar, Phillipe, Pablo and Flann. And a few finalists whose names remain unblemished: Kirk, Wanda, Ike, and Joyce.

"I like Kirk," shouts one intern.

Stone grabs his hair and spins a three-sixty with his body while still walking around the table, "*NO*, no-no-no. No fucking way. Kirk is terrible. Kirk is a rapist's name—

cross it off the list." An intern at the dry erase board strikes the name and considers certain odd tendencies of his cousin, Kirk.

"Okay, erase them—erase everyone but the last three. I want to see how they look." The group is on the fringe of breaking up hysterically at their tormented leader who is sinking under the weight of his impending forecast. They're also munching casually on some pizza and mozzarella sticks—in Stone's absence everyone smoked a J in the parking lot to calm down and also to spice up their creativity—news office activity code name: Team Building Exercise. The dry-erase intern obliterates the undesirable names from the board—he performs his duty in Vanna White style for the audience and earns a few whistles. "Way to go, Billy," a writer notes.

"Is this funny?" Stone asks, red-faced.

"No, I didn't mean to make a joke." The writer's pen quivers.

"That's right—it's no joke. You weren't there in '98. Goddamn highways like ice-skating rinks, back roads like bobsled courses..."

"*Stone*," she stops him, "I'm sorry, just calm down, let's try to relax." She hands him a mozzarella stick peace offering, which he smacks out of her hand—it splatters on the wall behind her. One intern cannot control his reaction to the odd thud made by the flying stick or the cheesy residue that seems to defy gravity in how slowly it slides down the wall. Stone lets the tension build as the room goes totally silent. They're all now focused on the giggling intern who, in his defense, is trying *so* hard not to laugh with his hand over his mouth and his head averted and red and everything.

"You like working here?" Stone asks him.

"Yeah," he spits out between giggles.

"Pick a name motherfucker."

"Joyce," he says.

"I like it," the writer says.

"Okay—Wanda it is," Stone says. "Erase the other names and let me look at her."

Vanna sweeps the names away to reveal the lone Wanda, in blue, thick and all capital against the white backdrop. Stone stares at the dry-erase board from across the room. Every employee sits between Wanda and weatherman. They look from one entity to the other. The silence grows strange and terrible. The only sound that of warm air humming through floor vents.

And still he stares.

Hmmmmm...

The giggling intern's cheeks swell—his face is near purple and balloonish. Everyone waits for him to burst. He must not look at the cheese.

And still, he stares.

Wanda.

Stone.

Wanda.

Stone.

"*Five...six...seven,*" Salazar pumps, "Yah, yah, grrrrr, uck, uhhnnnnn," he pumps, perhaps angrily, or truly dedicated, his veins are flaring from neck and biceps like a map of waterways all across his shaved chest. He stands up from the bench and likes the look of all this veinage in the mirror. He likes the way his brow hangs over his eyes. He likes the way two or three thick and moist and dark strands of his hair sweep across his long eyelashes. He likes the outline in his pants. He wants someone else to admire him and sends the following message to his ex fiancé:

I'm in our fuck room.

"And now for a look at the local weather let's send it over to our News Ten Meteorologist, Stone DeFoné."

"Thanks Darlene," Stone nods, approaching the camera. With his own chest puffed he walks so far beyond the X on the floor that his face dominates the entire shot—luckily his skin is clear and his tan is acceptable for February on Long Island, which is to say that he'd look out of place in Maine, or like a foreigner that local Brazilians would assume has been in town for about a week.

"Bad news, Long Island," he shakes his head, "bad, bad, news..." His face retreats to the map of the U.S.A. He positions his hands around a giant red, orange and yellow mass in a way that makes it seem like the meteorologist himself is moving the storm up the Eastern Seaboard. "You see this here," he says, cupping it, "this is Wanda."

The anchor looks over from her desk, Wanda.

Marco Salazar takes a break between sets and acknowledges, Wanda.

"I really thought he'd go with Joyce," giggles the intern.

"We've been tracking this system throughout the day with our News Ten Skytracker. We're in for it, Long Island. I'm predicting major accumulation and heavy, heavy icing. If surface temps stay low, as Triple Doppler indicates they will, we could be looking at the possibility of Cascade Failure."

"Cascade Failure?" asks Darlene, the anchor.

"Well, Darlene, think of dominos. When you knock the first one over, what happens next?"

"The rest will fall."

"That's right, very good. Now instead of dominos, picture power lines and trees."

"Oh *my*," says Darlene.

The camera pans back to Stone's face. He's way in front of the X again.

"Picture *this*, Darlene, Long Island: picture an entire frozen world stuck in Mother Nature's vise grip..." His hands squeeze the air in front of the camera. "Picture highways that are ice rinks. Picture back roads like bobsled tracks. Imagine unbearable cold and darkness, possibly for days..."

They're starting to lay down their pizza slices in the writers' room. Stone's face is stunningly close to the camera and everyone is wondering who the hell wrote this copy.

Marco chuckles at his old buddy between reps.

"My recommendation is to stay inside. Tune in for school closings with the morning weather. I'll have your first warning forecast by six."

"Thanks, Stone."

"Darlene?"

"Yes, Stone?"

"I have just one more thing to add."

"The floor is yours."

"I just," he looks down, loosens his tie for all to see and steps over the X, "I just want to remind everyone about Helga, the last great winter storm. That's the storm that made me want to become a meteorologist. That's the storm that cost my father his life. Patchogue residents," Stone wipes his mouth, "already know this story, but for everyone else, you'll remember that Jim Hurricane Schwartz, my predecessor, pleaded with people to stay off the roads, to close the schools—but they didn't listen, they opened the schools. You might think that meteorologists don't know what they're talking about, but Triple Doppler Radar and Skytracker are no joke. If a doctor tells you smoking causes cancer, do you doubt him and just go on smoking? You don't, but for some reason you doubted Hurricane, and you opened the schools. But then you saw what was happening, you felt that vise *grip*," he squeezes, "and you said okay...*now* let's get the kids home—but it was too late."

All the writers and interns are standing and staring at the television—their faces close and aglow in the screen, like Stone's at the camera.

Marco Salazar replaced his dumbbells on the rack. Hands on hips he looks at the TV, ignoring several surrounding mirrors.

Stone continues: "My dad, Boyle, was a school bus driver, one of the best. He didn't do anything wrong, he was just crossing an intersection when an SUV slid through a stop and T-Boned the bus he was driving. You might remember the story—the bus flipped on its side, he fell into the stairwell and crushed a child. I saw it happen. I was right there. Boyle lived, but you might say that he's never recovered. I'm telling you this now because we need to stay safe. We can't let another tragedy happen because we aren't prepared. I'm telling you this now because I need your help getting Boyle off the road. So *please*..." television screens all over Long Island are filled entirely by Stone's forehead, eyes, nose and mouth, "if you're in Patchogue," he's close enough that viewers see spittle land on the lens, he wipes his mouth and continues, "or any neighboring town, and you see a bus that shouldn't be driving around, it's probably my dad. Do whatever it takes to get him off the road and phone the News Ten hotline, immediately," a number flashes across Stone's forehead, "he'll probably just ask if you are going somewhere or want a ride, but don't listen to him. Please get him off that bus. I'm begging for your help, Long Island. Thank you."

"The ratings on this are gonna be huge," the writer says. "It's so personal."

"How's a *storm*...personal?" an intern asks.

"We fuckin' *name* them, don't we?"

"That's fair."

Marco flips off the TV, checks his phone: no reply from Melanie, no surprise there. So now it's time to bench. He walks over to the basement closet where all the stereo equipment is stored and places his favorite bench press disc onto the tray: Metallica's *Master of Puppets* is that album and he turns the volume up, slowly and gently, sniffing at it artistically like a violinist's first few strokes. He slides two plates on each side of the bar just as things start rocking and walks menacingly around to the front of the bench and sits. Instead of tilting back he stares at himself in the mirror: Master, master, where are the dreams that I've been after? Marco Salazar does finally fade back from the mirror and rips the bar from its holder. He takes a moment to admire the shape of his stressed arms, and when the hot young software man begins his vicious pump his heart charges along beating fresh blood that skates quickly through his circulatory system. His veins are stuffed and screaming, his brain pulsating under the weight—he's not even counting reps, just one after another after another. His face is hot and red, but when he looks down and sees how his chest is rippling he wants more. The incessant succubus pounding from the speakers aligns with the rhythm in Marco's chest and unlocks an unprecedented barbaric fury that presents itself as a sharp smile.

"Fuck."

"Fuck."

"Fuck yeah," he says and drops the weights back onto the rack with a bang. The software man unfolds his body from the bench and once again looks into all the mirrors. He tries his hair one way, and then another way—wants to see how it looks hanging over his forehead and also how it looks pulled back clean and parted over his right eye. In the midst of marveling at his extreme coolness, Marco's phone pops and he *runs* over to it. But it's only Lana:

Haven't heard from you tonight...hopefully that means you're getting your house ready for the party ;).

That smiling wink-face, she did that, it's extremely communicative. It's simultaneously forceful and knowing and passive aggressive—that wink is a takeover. It threatens Marco. This isn't really about an office party, now box up and erase the remains of your former life and make way *for me*. He replies: **NO** and throws his phone at the mirror, which for the first time ever he wishes had just been a normal wall—a double smash: phone, mirror, glass flying and cracking over the rack of dumbbells and onto the rubber matted floor.

A new track has just kicked into gear from the speakers and the software man doesn't want to hear it—his house is becoming less and less ready for a party. He pulls the whole rack of weights down onto the rubber floor and screams a song of anguish from the basement's inaudible reaches. Salazar goes again to the phone and sees that it's destroyed. He employs his entire musculature in an attempt to break the phone in half with his hands but can't, and this angers him further so he howls up high and fires the poor bit of electronics at another mirror, and so concludes the evening workout.

At this point, on a normal night, Marco Salazar would phone Lana to come over—but not tonight. Tonight he ventures one subterranean level further into his home. The wood stairway leading to his wine cellar spirals twice along rustic stone walls that, when touched, deliver a coolness that confirms one has journeyed beneath the earth's surface. This room did not exist when they bought the house but was constructed after the couple returned, just engaged, from Italy and France—they needed a place to store Melanie's Sommelierian haul. She even kept a tastevin down there, classy girl, to check wine quality in the appropriately dim cellar light. Probably three hundred bottles remained in boxes, and a hundred favorites were placed in surrounding racks—these vacant boxes were to be repurposed as storage and return receptacles for all the stuff Melanie had left behind—an activity Marco's been procrastinating for months, this packaging, this return, this end. Fuck *that*. He grabs a bottle of Brunello, and if you're wondering, or suspecting, then *yes*, he's got several bottles from when Biondi Santi was still doing his thing. This place, Montalcino, Tuscany, was somewhere they just *had* to go—a long way from Patchogue. She taught him everything about it—the aged grapes, Santi's refusal to go new school in his process, that his family basically *invented* this wine, all of it—she bounced in Italian cellars and flip-flopped through vineyards dangling the vines between her fingers. Marco uncorked the bottle and sniffed their old time. He went upstairs and swallowed her for hours.

He boxed nothing and slept alone.

Two towns over News Ten Meteorologist Stone

DeFoné sat stewing in front of a computer screen. He watched Wanda encroach on his territory. He sat there in the bare kitchen cracking his knuckles, hair on the loose, uncombed, pounding ales and dropping empties into an adjacent garbage can—not recycling and not sitting in a chair with any back support. He could hear the sound of intermittent air brakes circling throughout the night.

In the nether reaches of East Quogue, near the thundering commuter rail, the weasel refreshed and refreshed his office email. His itsy-bitsy mouse eyes drooped a fraction further with every pointless click until finally he slept upon his keyboard.

7

*W*ith no job or husband to speak of the slackened beast lady of Patchogue got roaring drunk most every night—this new dependence a devastating manifestation of the proud woman's inability to be independent. Crowds would gather outside the Salaznek home just to crow at her when she went to the store for smokes and booze—her son Mark still not quite old enough to get the supplies, though they'd tried to talk the store owner into it.

"He's going to take advantage of me, Claudia. That's what kids do. Next thing ya know he'll be buying booze for half the underage in town—I just can't have it."

And so she'd slide out the front door onto the porch and peck-peck-peck with her cane down the steps and peck-peck-peck with her cane down the block and back—hardly one bastard anywhere that would offer to carry her stuff when Mark wasn't around—somehow neighbors were more embarrassed to be seen helping her than not helping her. The name that everyone settled on was "Salack-neck". It hung lower and closer to her shoulder every month. Unsupervised children would whisper and taunt her with the word, staring the way only young kids can. Learning of her from older siblings had become a rite of passage. Adults would just ignore old Salack-neck and be damned if they were about to scold somebody else's shitty kid.

Young Marky came to dread returning home to find his mother in the same slumped position—up against the left side of the couch, full mothering weight applied to the bulimicly thin, foam-puking cushion, drunkenly immobilized, impossible to tell if she'd passed out or waited up for him.

"Wudja been playin' on dem cumpooters at skool all nigh again?"

"Yeah," he'd reply—getting an immediate sense in his nostrils that it was time to empty her bedpan.

"Alwaze on dem pooters, playin' on dem cumpooters," she'd chuckle and cough, "I needa bath, Margy."

She'd hold an arm out for him to grab and lead upstairs. In the tight stairway he could smell Claudia's decline—wet putrid feet recently removed from sweaty sewage socks baked with onions and garlic in a hot summer apartment. Ten baths couldn't wash away this reeking. Sometimes he could taste the funk on his teeth. This scent of withering dominated the entire home.

Each day, on his way home and before his dreaded re-entry, Mark looked into people's windows. You know the scene: warm lighting, meals, hugs, Mom dusting windowsills and lampshades all weekend. A breath of familiar air—blueberry muffins by the fire, summer orthodontics camps, a safe haven from taunting and ridicule. These other homes looked gentle, like the swaddle of clean linens that Mark dreamed about. But instead he woke in the chokehold of his own home, more like an enclosure, the base definition of shelter with a sick grip—nonsense piled up in all corners of *that* house and crept like quicksand from fringes to the middle of rooms threatening to eventually overtake the residents—empty cigarette packs and bottles acted as calendars, unread magazines spilled from end tables onto the floor and nestled against porcelain trinkets grouped like a collection of late night subway passengers—you know, dancing ballerinas, a clown holding balloons, a doggy, a small Chinese girl, a sly alabaster fox looking to rob a jewelry box Claudia had opened and mumbled over one night, mail everywhere that she'd never opened, her emergency toilet paper just visible beneath the blankets by the cot and bedpan. Filth such as this festers over time in a manner epitomized by military tactics—it oppresses and outnumbers, its daily presence and stench suffocate the opponent who feels hopeless, depressed and entirely unable to fight back. Entering the Salaznek home one would fully expect to find a few caged squirrels hanging around the back rooms.

And upstairs her combs and brushes lay all around the sink with a million long orange hairs writhing in the thin coat of water that leaked always from the faucet. Claudia would even lay her toothbrush and their floss in the hairy water—from the bathroom a colossal pile of clothes could be seen through a crack in her bedroom door and some evidenced an occasional inability to reach the bedpan in time. On one such occasion Claudia went upstairs to change from her dirty drawers because she needed to go to the store and had too much pride to go like *that*. She positioned her body on the edge of the bed. With her left side leaning up against the headboard she one-handedly flung the soiled drawers down to the ground and looked at them, thinking about her life now. She grabbed the new panties previously positioned to her right and floated them in the air, letting them dangle down by her foot as though she were fishing or teasing a kitten. Getting her right foot through the right foot hole wasn't the worst, the left was more difficult—it regenerated, some, through massaging and some new electric pulsing, but not really enough to be described as functional—and certainly not spry. She slid the underwear up a bit. Using her right calf as a tether she stretched the fabric toward her left foot. She tried to move the foot up enough to simply slide the foot through and put her underwear on but the foot wouldn't go that high. Now playing the role of fish, not fisherman, she flopped back on the bed hoping that gravity would pull the leg up enough to get through the tethered undies. The left foot did come up *some* with that initial flop, but not enough. Again, launching from the right foot she built up momentum each time her head bounced off the mattress and back to an upright position. Always maintaining the tether between calf, elastic waistband and hand, she launched...and launched...her orange hair flapping up through the air each time like that of a bikini model emerging from the ocean. She flung her body back and forth three more times, one...and a...two, her back beating the bed like the last three pumps of sex, and finally all her weight and momentum brought the left leg vertically into the air—quickly, with her right hand stretching toward her left foot (most would consider just one position of any enjoyable Sunday yoga session), and the left foot floating in limbo like a hitchhiker, Claudia Salaznek wrapped the elastic around the left ankle and flopped from her head back up once again to sitting position, which allowed her to slip the garment all the way up to her hip. She smiled. Pants were always easier, they're stiff and big and they stay in place—you can work with 'em, it's not a one shot deal.

Propelled by her first sense of accomplishment in months, Claudia thought she'd just go back downstairs like any other cane-carrying person—and so not sliding down on her butt one step at a time like usual. She didn't make it two steps. She'd not considered the weight adjustment, and like a stumped weightlifter dumping the one side forgets all the weight on the other is going to violently pull them the other way, Claudia put her cane ahead, down onto the first step, and when she stepped down with her right foot, all her weight went that way, because there was no counterbalance with the slackened left side. She bounced down the steps like a bowling ball, eventually coming to rest in the compact Salaznek foyer.

Mark got home two hours later and the damn door wouldn't open. He shoved it a second time with a shoulder and an audible grunt, "What the fuck is it now?" he said, assuming Claudia might be playing a prank.

"Mom, open the door," he yelled and slammed his hand on it, bang-bang-bang.

"Uckkkk, Imunder-earrrrr."

"MOM?"

"MARGY, helb-ime under earrrr."

Mark tiptoed right against the window to look inside but saw nothing. Then the right hand fingers shot up into his vision, as if from the grave. "Mom!" he acknowledged, and ran around to the back of the house.

"I can't rrreally moov. I fell," she said, stuck between the front door and first stair.

"Hang on, I'm gonna call Officer Gerard."

Mark lifted his mother off the floor and brought her to the couch. He sponged some blood from her forehead while they waited. "What happened, Ma?"

"I jus fell. Gedmee a cigured wudja?"

He hands her the smoke—lights it for her first, then hands it to her. "You're not supposed to be going up and down the stairs without me, Ma."

"Baai-know. I was feelin' gud, so I jus went furrit."

Claudia Salaznek was hospitalized for two days following this underwear incident. This seemed an opportune time for Mark to throw a party and maybe make some friends and who knows, maybe even get laid for the first time—at least that's what his buddy Stone figured.

That Friday the young DeFoné, who no one wanted to fuck with (he's *crazy*—his dad's *fucking nuts* too), spread word to his Freshman and Sophomore pals that his friend Mark had an open house and was throwing a banger. "Dude you mean Salack-neck?" "Yeah, he's a good guy," Stone replied, threateningly. Stone coped with his messed-up-parent attention much differently than Mark did. Mark went the way of the loner, not wanting to confront or be confronted. Stone confronted every single person that may or may not have said the slightest derogatory thing about his driving dad. He screamed and yelled, he raged, he punched and bloodied his way to acceptance—he beat the unkindness out of their ignorant faces.

Everything went well enough at first. People just lingered shyly around Mark's small backyard sipping from beer and wine and bottles they all brought—joints passed around, some stoners tripping kindly on mushrooms—wandering in and out of the deep woods behind Mark's house—just a party of teens handling their anxiety. As it turned out, a different party, a party for The Seniors, got broken up, and one of those acned bastards called his little brother to see what was up. They drove over in their cars—they knew how to get actually drunk and they were. They didn't see that everyone was in the backyard so they walked right through the front door and smelled the smell. They saw the beige disaster sitting there all foamless. They saw the magazines and figurines and mail. They saw the living room cot and adjacent bedpan. They hissed the cats away and moved into the kitchen and grabbed Claudia's whiskey and started passing that around. They saw the ashes piled up and lit their own cigarettes. They disregarded the ashtrays entirely.

"This place is fucking *nasty*," one of The Seniors said.

They looked through the refrigerator for some food and found none, laughed at this, joked, "What are they putting on all those dirty ass dishes?"

"What's the point of having dishes when you don't have any food?" another one said, examining a dish in front of his face. Then he smashed it down on the kitchen floor. This act of defiance stiffened their chapped little dicks. Standing in a wide circle they looked at each other like the thing they had discovered was gravity—they all wanted to experiment, with the dishes. And when they ran out of dishes they went into the cupboard for the glasses. And when the glasses were done they went for the ashtrays and empty highballs—not the first glass smashed around this kitchen certainly, but more unwelcome. Stone burst through the back door to the rescue and cocked one of The Seniors in the face—he absolutely *blasted* him—it made that bad sound that makes witnesses nervous in the stomach. That dude dropped bloody to the ground. His two buddies closest to the living room ran for the front door. Stone caught the last one by the jacket and pulled him back into the kitchen with such force that he slipped on the glass. Stone was on top of him pretty quickly and started pounding away. What form—a lot of rights, just unloading. Between thuds the guy on the ground put his feeble hands in the air and made noises that sounded like "Stop," or "Please," but Stone didn't give a shit about that. His hair was all over the place in front of his eyes, no semblance of the night's early combing—his face fire alarm red and matching the blood flowing from the other guy's nose.

Stone's first target came to and shoved the future weatherman off his friend then picked up his bloody buddy and ran for the front door. DeFoné sat on all the cracked glass laughing hysterically at the two cowards who, in retreat, decided to kick over the living room bedpan. "*Ah*, it's shit and *piss*," one said, seemingly expecting something else to spill from a bedpan. "Nasty fuggin' Salack-necks," uttered the other, plugging his bloody nose with his own fingers. Once outside they thought it would be a good time to kick one of the two rickety porch columns to hell, and wouldn't you believe that the roof over the front porch did not collapse but tilted at an incredible downward angle—to the left. For good measure they uprooted the Dwarf Alberta and chucked it onto the porch steps leaving a disturbing mixture of soil and woodchips in their wake.

The rest of the crowd, attracted by the commotion,

entered the house and discovered Stone laughing. He was up now, slickly leaning against a countertop and slurping Claudia's whiskey straight from the bottle—showing off his battered knuckles.

"Somebody gimme a cigarette," Stone said coolly, though he'd never smoked one before.

"What's that smell?" a really cute Colombian girl asked.

Mark was last to enter. The cute Colombian girl turned to him and asked, "You actually like...*live* here?"

"Yeah."

"You guys need to clean your house. It's gross," she said, pinching her face together.

"Fuck you," Mark replied.

"Thatta boy," Stone added.

"Get the fuck out then," Mark told her, a bit drunk.

"Oh my God, is that fucking *shit* on the floor?" She pointed.

Five of her friends kind of screamed and put their hands on their cheeks. "Ewwww, it *is* shit."

The dudes were too afraid of Stone to say shit about the shit. He looked them over to make sure that not one person said anything even remotely derogatory about the Salaznek house.

But the girls went on calling out cruel farewells about ole Salack-neck. They ran for the front door toward the echo of Senior engines, hoping for a ride. They didn't have the balls to run under the tilted roof or jump the Dwarf Alberta that lay across the steps, so of course they turned around, walked back through the living room, whispering about the couch before quitting it in the kitchen—they walked in a quiet line, young dudes followed the girls out the back door, the only sound feet bashfully crunching glass. Stone yelled, "*Fuck* you!" and lunged his face at the whole crowd, which made them jump and scoot out the door.

And so the two studs were left alone standing in what remained of the kitchen. Mark still a virgin, and Stone

DeFoné bleeding all over the floor.

Stone passed the bottle of whiskey. Mark took a good snort of it.

"Fuck 'em, forget about 'em," Stone said.

Then the boys got drunk together. They sat on the couch with the bottle and puffed down a whole pack of Claudia's Marlboros, coughing all the way. They shared stories about the thing that first brought them together—the thing that outcast them, strange mishaps, strange parents. And in each other's drunken company, the company of an unfortunate twin, they could laugh and joke about their parents' acquired deformities. They slurred their speech like Claudia's. Stone sat on the couch and mimed the bus door open and employed his Salack-voice to ask the familiar, "Goin' sumwairrrr?" Mark brought the stereo from his room and introduced DeFoné to Cobain for the first time—showed him his air guitar and told him about Kurt's downfall. Stone could see the passion with which young Mark spoke. He watched how his hands worked, how he sat on the very edge of the couch and looked straight at Stone's face when he talked about concerts he'd gone to in the city—about the programming work he'd done to afford it, at sixteen, setting up sites for small businesses all over Long Island. Mark told Stone about the shit he'd seen in New York, all the people, how none of *this* (he pointed to the glass and couch and porch) will end up mattering that much. Stone shed his macho façade and spoke about his own passion, the weather: "That's why I love weather, it's so fucking unpredictable, it fucking *kills*, man—just like me."

"Wouldn't your job be to predict the weather though?" From a young age it was clear that Mark was really the smart one. Eventually, after sweeping the glass, shit and piss into garbage bags, the boys arrived at a transcendent realization: Claudia, already dangerous behind the wheel, probably wouldn't be able to drive when she got home. Mark told Stone how insane it was when he did ride with her—her entire left side rested against the driver's window and door. Mark had no clue how she made right turns. He imitated the situation for his pal. He theorized that the sun blinded her left eye during long portions of their Monday trips to the fish market.

"Dude, you go to the market on *Monday*?"

"No one's around there on Monday."

"You're a smart fuck, aren't you?"

"Right, so maybe we could all hop on the bee? Is it?"

"Yeah."

"We could all hop on the bee when my mom gets home tomorrow, and Boyle can drive us and they'll both be happy."

"You *are* a smart fuck."

It didn't take good Officer Gerard's mustache long to figure out what went down at the Salaznek house in Claudia's absence.

"Those fuggers," Claudia said, noticing her prized Spruce laid out on the porch steps. Gerard escorted her from the cruiser and up the front walkway. Motioning to the collapsing porch roof and missing column, he said, "I know some guys that'll come by and take care of that for you, Mrs. Salaznek."

"Thank yoo Juhrrad."

"Wadda fuck Margy?" Claudia asked, entering the house.

"I'm sorry, Ma. I had some people over..."

"Fuggem Margy, issokay, issokay. I geddit." She touched his head.

"What happened, Mark?" asked Gerard.

"Issokay Juhrrad...I can tackit frommearrr."

Gerard looked around, like cops always do, his lips smooching at the scene from all angles just below his mustache—and above the mustache his nostrils heaved at the vile miasma quickly accumulating in the thick black bristles. He made a sound with his mouth like, "*Mau*-god," and touched his blue brim, trying to act cool—

undisgusted. Three cats purred around the feet of the official stranger. Being a good cop, Gerard figured the brownness around their lips was not cat lipstick. The foul living room aroma continued to gather and muster nastily in Gerard's mustache. His moistening eyes betrayed the calm exterior. He felt dizzy and poisoned by the foreign toxins. He wanted to help, but he had to puke. People shouldn't have to live like this...

"You don't have to stay," Mark told him.

"You folks let me know if you ever need anything else, okay? I'll send someone over to take care of that porch, all right?"

"Thanks Officer," Mark said, nodding, meaning it.

"Sure thing..." He tipped his blue cap. And left quickly.

From the kitchen Claudia called, "Wherrrzall my glazzes Margy?"

"Well..."

"An my whizgy. Wherrrz my whizgy Margy? Those *fuggers*!"

"Me and Stone drank the whiskey, Mom."

"Endjaa shmoge my cigaress too?"

"Yeah."

"Fuggers," she grinned, "les go to dastorr."

PUH-*FOOSH*.

"Wuz that?"

"Got a surprise for you, Mom. A welcome home present."

"I wuz harrrdly gone."

Mark helped Claudia to the front door. Stone DeFoné was already outside trying to work the Spruce back into the ground.

"Hey, Miss Salaznek," he said.

"Hello der Stone. Leave that therrr furrnow wudja?"

"Okay, Miss Salaznek. Are you all right?" Stone stood up, pointed at the bandage around her head.

"I jus fell izall. Thangs fur askin'."

Claudia saw Boyle DeFoné waiting patiently inside his

bus. "Wuz thisall about?"

"Got us a chauffeur to the market today."

"Welllll den lugget us," she said, delight lifting the right side of her face.

Mark, Stone, and Claudia walked into the driver's field of vision and waited for the sign to cross. Boyle checked the rearview and the sideview and the other sideview. He also checked for oncoming traffic. All clear, he waved them to cross and they did so at Claudia's caned pace.

"Goin' somewhere?" Boyle asked, unfolding the doors.

Mark ushered his mother up the stairwell. She slumped into the seat behind Boyle and leaned against the window. Her son sat down next to her. Bad memories of this bus, but not today. A shining Monday sun heated the plastic seats. The warm glass felt pleasant against Claudia's face. She used the bandage on her forehead to clear the drool off the window. As the bus rolled through Old Brookville Mark shuffled out of the seat with Claudia and into the row behind her. He pinched the plastic pieces together and slid his creaking bus window down all the way. He stuck his nose out the window like a dog. Claudia spoke into the glass: "Wud izit Margy?" But he ignored her. It was, *ah*, Old Brookville. Not just a scent from an open window but an *ah-atmosphere*. The cool presence of freedom—freedom from morning and evening flabby calf massages, from disabled and deserting parents, from living room funk. Freedom from even *the word* worry—the stuff sifting into that bus wasn't fresh air but elegance spiked with mint cannabis and chased with Spanish Rioja. All's quiet, you can just sit there listening to birds. The mothers of Old Brookville walk on tanned feet, just front-yarding it in white pants all day long while holding hands with their blonde bonneted babes. Destination? Oh, I don't know, nowhere really, maybe down to the beach, or stop at Fred's to pick up *something*. They smile so white and wave to the sweating men perpetually raking and mowing these yards.

Mark noticed one mother shelter the ears of her child

as the bus rumbled past. (The noise from the air brakes did rudely pierce the otherwise perfect atmosphere.)

Boyle announced, "The bumble bee bus goes buzz, buzz, buzz..."

"Jesus Dad."

"...all through the towwwwnnnnnnn."

Claudia enjoyed the tune, certainly, swinging her maestro hand back and forth above the seat to the rhythm while serenading her warm window, "Buzzzbuzzzbzzz." As the mansions of Old Brookville receded the earth flipped open her convertible top to reveal the entire sky flashing forever blue over the ocean. The breeze kicked up and shot through their traveling tube bringing with it the Monday market odor to which Stone responded, "*Dude*," and Mark slid up his window.

If you don't already know, Monday is not the day to buy fish. What is still on sale Monday is leftover from Friday, Saturday, and Sunday. Anything mongers move on Monday is just a bonus. Those fish are rank. They smell like their gaping mouths and bulging eyes look, puking at the thought of lying around in the sun for so long. Monday shoppers share knowing glances with each other. However, the fearsome foursome rolled off the bus not caring about any of that. Mrs. Salaznek walked in front— the bandaged leader, cane-bobbing her way to some tasty deals. Ninety-seven seagulls circled overhead, caw-caw-cawling for everyone to stay away from their dinner and sometimes even dropping claiming grenades upon the decaying fare.

"Fugging burrs," Claudia said, lighting up a Marlboro.

From a distance the platters of aligned fish fins look like potential beach house wallpaper, a feast in wait. The hungry friends humped on down peacefully before the characteristically crass fishwife took notice. "Well, look at this motley crew." Several other shoppers turned to look.

The fishmonger snapped, "Would you *shush*, those two come every Monday."

"And you think I don't know that, you dumb bastard?"

"Hiya ya fuggin' bitch Molly," Claudia said, caning her way to the table.

"How ya doing Mrs. Salaznek? What the hell happened to you? Ya try and go jogging again?"

"This place is *da bes*," Claudia said, turning to Stone and Boyle. "Thave da bes fishearrr." Stone nodded his head, not sure if he should say something to the fishwife.

"Jus fell izall."

"Hello, Claudia," said the fishmonger, coming over. He removed a thick black glove from his right hand to shake Claudia's. With her left occupied (cane) and right with cigarette, Claudia had to put the smoke in the right side of her lips and hold it there to make way for the fishmonger's greeting. Flies swarmed from the fish to her hair, encircling the dry orange mess shining in the sun. When she got her hand back she swatted at the flies with the cigarette still hanging from her mouth.

"Hi Dairy," she said. "Wuz goodearrr tuday?"

"Well," said Terry, looking around, anywhere but at her mouth, "the catfish fillets aren't bad."

Mark stood apart from the deal. He let Claudia have her time—he wasn't ever sure how much she really liked fish but she loved the way they treated her at the market. Mark wasn't sold. They tried so hard to treat her normally that it betrayed their obvious awareness of her abnormality and made him feel worse.

"Dey holdup tooda heat pretty gudden?"

"Molly," the fishmonger called, "bring over the catfish."

"She can wait," yelled the fishwife.

"Wadda bitch," Claudia said, "I really luvverr."

When Molly did come with the fillets she stopped to grab a bag of something on ice stashed under one of the tables. "I caught these this morning—saved 'em for you, Claudia. Thought you might be coming by today."

"Wudda ya got?"

"Fresh oysters."

"Ya fuggin' wid me? Orrstuhrs on uh Monday?"

"Just for you ya cripple. Now quit running around and maybe I'll go out and snatch something for you next week too."

"Margy!"

Mark walked over with his wallet out to pay, "What'd ya get, Ma?"

"Bagga orrstuhrs."

"Oysters on a Monday?" Mark asked, looking more at Molly.

"I went out and caught 'em myself this morning, ya smart little prick."

Claudia held the bag out for her son to take. Mark passed it back to his buddy Stone, still hungover, a bit nauseated, but excited by the prospect of oysters.

"Waddid I tell ya? This place is da bess, da *bess*. I tell errrybuddy dadull lissen," Claudia said loud enough that folks took notice. You could tell they didn't all feel the same, or they didn't understand her. Either way, they weren't as happy to be there. They thought *this* smell was bad...some had their lips pursed out so far in the air that they appeared more disapproving than the fish.

"Fuckin' retard," someone whispered.

Stone had him in a flash. He pulled the man's shirt collar back so his eyes looked straight into the sun until Stone's face blotted it out: "What'd you just say?" he asked.

"Nothing," the man chirped, dropping a fish onto the pavement.

"You *sure*?" Stone asked, face all red.

"I didn't say *shit*. I'm sorry."

Stone let him up. "That's what I thought." He followed his friends to the bus without ever letting go of the oysters.

In the bus, away from the market, the fish actually smelled fresh. A few choice citizens set free from the mountain of corpses put things into delicious perspective. Claudia held the bag of fillets in her lap. The sun burned into her leaning left eye. Mark hoped she closed it, a prolonged wink. He noticed the right side of her face in full smile, satisfied, dimple and all. Boyle DeFoné led everyone in song, "Buzz-buzz-buzz, all through the town," and Mark did buzz, and Stone did buzz, half-heartedly, like the way young children sing in church. Ah, what a group, a gang of pirates returning home with some sweet bounty and greeted by two sweaty gentlemen banging away at the Salaznek porch. They'd reestablished the rickety column. They'd repainted where it split. They had ladders and brooms and tool bags hanging about the porch and tool belts full of tools draped around their waists.

"Well, look at this motley crew," one said, watching them exit the bus.

Claudia peck-peck-pecked up the front walk, sizing up the rebuild. "Well dat lucks puh-ritty guuud," she said.

"Thanks, Claudia," the scruffier older one said. The one who, when he was the younger one's age, never thought he'd still be doing odd jobs around the neighborhood.

"Uggay Mikey, you boys hungrrry den?"

"We wouldn't want to impose," Mikey said, rubbing his trim stomach.

"Come on, it's the least we can do," said Mark.

"What'd'ya get?" Mikey asked.

"Catfish fillets and some oysters."

"Oysters on a Monday?"

"Mawly cawdum tudday, fresh jus furrr me," Claudia said.

Mark sent Mikey to the corner store with a twenty for plates, cups and Marlboros. Stone fired up the grill and Boyle watched in amazement as everyone moved so quickly around him. When Mikey got back, Claudia put some oyster ice into the plastic cups and pulled a secret bottle of whiskey from the cupboard, "Thisizzz from Dick's ole stash," she told everyone, "I was savin' it for a speshull uggazian." She handed cups out to the workers and her son and to Stone as well. They passed around the

Marlboros too. They turned up the radio Mikey had there on the porch. Mikey's assistant Vinny shucked the oysters with a flathead screwdriver to rousing applause—they had no other tool. "Lucky for you I grew up on the docks," Vinny said, and truly they did feel that way. These aren't the people you see at brunch wearing white with designated squeezing lemons and cocktail sauce and dwarf forks and whatnot—these porch people put straight Tabasco sauce on the oysters and suck 'em down with the whiskey and chase it with Marlboro drags. They spoke generally of motherfuckers and bullshit above paper plates. Sets of neighbors power-walked by, trying to enjoy the summer sunset in their own way—their elbows flared wide in an effort to speed past the porch. Fearful of being heckled they whispered to each other, "I don't know what it *is* with those people, just sitting out on the porch like *that*."

When the sun did finally tuck its forehead behind the freshly repaired roof, all the gentlemen stepped down from the porch to the yard. Claudia sat smoking by the radio. The left strap of her tulip tank top rested in the crease of her elbow, where it had been for the past three hours. She leaned back against her home and watched them go to work, cane idly aside, feet outstretched in front of her. Mark and Stone pulled a deep trench in the soil with their bare hands. Mikey and Vinny dusted off the dense needles and stretched out some roots. Boyle could hardly believe what was happening. Mikey and Vinny placed the tiny Spruce back into the ground and held it there while Mark and Stone packed it tight with dirt. Then Mikey and Vinny joined the boys on the ground. The four of them, on their hands and dirt-stained knees, packed the tree and patted the ground from all sides until the Dwarf Alberta stood tall and firm, poking stiffly into the air once again.

8

Salazar's eyelids flash open suddenly, as if from a coma. He groans, the stretching at the center of his CK's reminds him that he is alone. He occupies a tiny corner of his king-size bed. No Melanie. No Lana—just Marco and the receptionist (adult film star). For the first time in a while the software stud can actually hear the spicy spacebrew gurgling before he smells it. For the first time in a while he must tackle the morning hard-on himself. It must be seven-seventeen, he thinks, watching the receptionist bend for the phone. "Hello," she says. The scene cuts to the boss's office: "Ginger, get in here...I've got a big package that needs to be taken care of immediately." Ginger enters the office, looking around, "Where's the big package?" she asks, innocently. The boss circles around the desk and displays the big package, "Right here," he says. Yeah, it's right here, Marco thinks. Feeling empowered the software man leaps from the empty bed, "It's right here," he says. "Who's the boss," he says, stroking, standing so close to the screen you'd think he was trying to get a whiff. Nearing the end, Marco recalled a time in the basement with Melanie pressed against the mirrors. He pressed himself into the screen. He pushed his sharp forehead against the wall. "Yeah, it's right...*here*," he said, finishing on the screen.

Now prepared to live this day to its fullest, like it might be his last, Marco pours a cup and flips on the television. News Ten is showing a dastardly montage of cars sliding everywhere—into telephone poles, into trees, into each other. The sheen on the roads appears so supernaturally slick it must have been enhanced by editorial at Stone's behest—really driving home the dangers of glaze. These cars don't dance to a tune; they spin to the silence of a winter storm that wreaks havoc on the nerves until each collision's cacophonic finale. Then brief images of men at each other's throats in front of five-car pileups. The men wear no caps on their balding heads. Purple down jacket in one corner versus orange down jacket in the other, light denims and dark boots, utterly unadvisable winter fashion. These men were pissed before the storm (you rarely find the well dressed in any kind of public tussle, especially one filmed for instructional purposes). A narrator advises, "In any winter storm it is important to be patient and remain calm." Here you'd perhaps like to see at worst a traffic jam suggestive of a patient yet safe homeward commute, and at best a family in front of a fire, sipping tea, still with power, just waiting for the big bear to blow over. But instead the montage cuts to a helicopter crashing nearly on top of a man hammering away at a telephone pole for whatever reason—couldn't either of them have waited until tomorrow? Would things have been better if the chopper pilot had been more patient and calm? The whole instructional shebang closes with the sound of a (post-production) terrified scream as the chopper crashes in the snow. With the fluffy stuff flying everywhere, the repairmen jumps from his perch, and the narrator concludes, "One can never be sure where or when disaster will strike," perhaps winking at the unlikely scenario.

The camera cuts to a close-up of News Ten

Anchorwoman Umi Culvida: "Now let's take you right back to Meteorologist Stone DeFoné in the Weather Center for the very latest on this developing storm."

"Yeah, right," Marco says, slurping his spacebrew.

"Wow Umi, *real* scary video there. Good morning and thanks for joining us here at News Ten Long Island. I think we can all see that it does not take much ice to lead to serious problems. That's why, with major accumulation on the way in the next few hours, it's wise, if at all possible, to just stay inside."

"Okay," Marco says.

Stone retreats to the big map that once contained the entire U.S.A. but is now dominated by Long Island. "If we take a look at Triple Doppler Radar we can see the cold air funneling down from the north, up by East Quogue and along the coast..." Blotches ranging in color from green all the way to purple crawl like irrational amoebas all over Long Island. Each color is labeled in the key at the bottom left corner of the screen where green through yellow equals rain before turning to blue (snow/ice) then purple, which represents "mix," though exactly how that differs from "snow/ice" is never made clear. Then the key changes to represent wind patterns and Stone swings his arm to follow the eastbound gusts. Blowing air with his lips, he emphasizes, "It's going to get extreeemely windy as the day progresses." Universal wind symbols pepper the map; replacing the amoebas, they dot the whole island. Stone turns to the camera with a look of dread, "When this group of high pressure clouds arrives, the precipitation will pass quickly through the layer of warm above-freezing air here in the upper region before getting super cooled by today's frigid surface temperatures. I wore this white suit as a visual reference and reminder for you, Long Island, it's gonna be Ice-Ice, *baby*, all day long. I'm now fairly certain we have a Glaze Event on our hands. This Wanda is gonna be one cold B—woman."

"Oh *my*," the camera cuts back to Umi, "News Ten will

be sure to keep you updated on school closings and traffic conditions throughout the day."

"We sure will—we're camping out here in the Weather Center. And Umi..."

"Yes, Stone?"

"I'd just like to remind everyone again that if they see my father Boyle driving around to please, *please* do anything in your power to get him off the roads, or at least phone the News Ten hotline so I can get out there myself." The number flashes on the screen again.

"And *Stone*, before you run off?"

"Yes, Umi?"

"Do you have a fun fact for us today, or have you cancelled it again?"

"Oh sh—, yeah, that's right, sure I do. I got this one from our Money Watch Team. Last year the number of Americans who drink coffee fell from sixty-six percent to sixty-one, back to you." He points.

"*Well*," Umi laughs as she's supposed to, "that certainly sounds like bad news for Starbucks. Wonder what that's all about Todd?"

"Fascinating," mocks the male co-anchor, Todd Michaels, reasonably jealous of Stone's white suit or frustrated by the way his co-anchor's insistence on wearing red mutes his otherwise spectacular February tan, "maybe the Money Watch Team should invest in *tea*," he adds.

Satisfied with Stone's forecast, Marco heads to work. He ashes through the sunroof and checks his appearance in the rearview: his dark hair is combed, parted, and matches the black of his leather jacket. And that leather matches the black leather seats, and this leather euphoria does give off a beastly smell, ripe and invigorating in the raw morning. Sadly, surrounding clouds offset Marco's moneyed vibe, a hanging display of potential meteorological accuracy.

The 2s are pressed together in the Egostatistical parking lot awaiting the arrival of their alleged oppressor.

They're huddled for warmth, so tightly that they actually appear to be one entity—a single jacketed mass. There is a man in the middle of the group with a head so thin his winter cap hangs loosely over his ears. If someone were to invent a winter cap with a drawstring, he'd be first in line—the best thing for him is a child's headband or earmuffs, but he refuses. He says, "*Hola*, Juan Miguel." And Juan Miguel replies, "*¿Hola Jorge, que pasa?*" Jorge begins to whisper something to Juan Miguel, but before he can finish everyone turns to look up the road. The 2s' bellies bunch with nerves when they hear the familiar howling engine. They disperse to retrieve their signs from the tundra. Jorge jogs away from the cluster as the polished car rolls into the lot. They jerk the signs up and down with admirable vigor. Marco sees their mouths opening and closing and can sense bellowing but he's blasting the rock n roll. When he gets out he hears the yelling but as usual can't understand. He does not notice the office weasel running for the front door.

"*¡Que te jodan!*"

"*¡Púdrete en el infierno!*"

"*¡Eres un mierda!*" The 2s shout.

From his trunk Marco gathers ten, twelve, even twenty sets of Gore-Tex brand gloves, and umbrellas to boot. He passes all this necessary stuff to the 2s.

"It's about to start icing all over your asses," he says.

"Ju jes want us to put down these *signs*, mang," Juan Miguel yells, "Chyeahhhhh," chants the huddled mass behind him, adding various insults en Español. They leave the gloves and umbrellas on the ground.

"Your breath reeks of champagne, Juan. I trust you and Junior had a fabulous evening?"

"Ju can jes go inside and *fuck* jorself, mang," Juan retorts.

"I bet you'd like it if I went inside, wouldn't you, Juan?"

Juan makes no reply. The shouting mass says enough.

"Suit yourselves, but I'm warning you, it's about to get really nasty out here."

Most of the 2s aren't sure what Marco's saying. The weasel's already begun to whip himself into frenzy. He slaps his jacket down onto his swivel chair upon entering the office and shouts, "What a day," while throwing his arms in the air for punctuation. On his way into the kitchen he stretches the collar of his horrible orange button-down shirt and cranes his neck to the side mumbling about the craziness of something. Shawn gives Leah a 'you fucking believe this guy?' look—being George's neighbors in the open office environment they'd begun to develop a theory about the collar in relation to the winter cap. They surmised that, seeing the way his hat hangs so loose over his head—like a guy who'd borrowed a condom from the wrong roommate—he sports the tight collars to reinforce his own significance, and to prove that his humanity is relevant enough to fill fabrics.

George paces around the office while waiting for his cappuccino to brew. The office is unusually quiet, and the weasel's grievances are heard from front to back: "Are we really gonna stay here all day, this is crazy, crazy, *crazy*. Every school is closed. I swear no one else is working today." His complaints go generally unnoticed. He's peeping at the computer screens of absent employees. He pretends to be so worked up over the weather that he slips into a few mousepads or keyboards and wakes these computers from their slumber—he's hoping someone left their computer on and office email open so he can fully read the email about the party at Marco's—he doesn't know the address, or what time to be there.

"George, your cappuccino is ready," Lana calls from the office kitchen.

"Boss comin' in today?"

"He sure is. I got an email from him last night actually."

"An email?" George cranes his neck at Lana, stirring even more sugar into his frothy cappuccino. "What about?" he asks, casually.

"Something about his phone breaking and him needing me to have a new one for him today."

"Oh, *that* all?"

"Yep."

"That's it?" George asks. Gripping his minimug and *not* taking a saucer he tilts his head oddly at the executive assistant. He studies her from head to toe in that rude way men are rarely aware of, never considering how inappropriately long it takes to reach conclusions like: she looks great in heels but her shirt is too tight—something he can relate to.

"Yes, George, that's it."

"Do you think we'll get out early today?"

"Not sure. Nothing's coming down yet."

"Maybe we should *all* just leave and have a big party, or something," George says, looks at the ceiling.

Just then the elevator doors glide open and Marco Salazar enters the office—leather jacketed, travel mug of spacebrew, striding with sleek shoulder bag he runs his right hand through the thick moist black locks of hair and turns his deep gaze to Lana's desk, but she's not there.

"HEYYOOO, boss is here," the weasel yells. He fires out from the kitchen pinching his minimug between thumb and forefinger and stretching his collar from the Adam's apple. He comments, "*Nice* jacket."

Marco ignores the compliment and hurries into his office, closes the door, waits for Lana.

"Here," she says, entering, presenting the new phone.

"Thanks."

"So, that email you sent was pretty weird."

"What?"

"There were like ten typos in it, Marco."

"See, I'm lost without you."

"Were you drunk?"

"That's none of your business."

"Okay... How'd your phone break then?"

Marco pretends to be getting some work started. Lana becomes aware of lingering.

"Is your house ready for the party?" She asks after a minute.

"Cancel the party."

"Is something wrong, Marco?" she asks, seeking results and details in the results-driven, detail-oriented environment.

"I didn't feel like boxing up all her stuff, if that's what you're really asking."

"Why not?"

"I just didn't."

"*Why*? She fucking hates you Marco, remember—she said that, she thinks you're sick. She gave the ring back."

"I don't want to talk about this now."

"Fine. Do you really want me to cancel the party though?"

"Yeah, but it's not that. I don't think people should be driving around tonight. Did you see the weather report?"

"I was already on my way into work."

"It's gonna be bad."

"You just don't want everyone getting stuck at your house."

"It looks like half the office stayed home anyway."

"They emailed, mostly the moms—said they had to stay home and watch the kids."

"No sweat."

"They also said they could still make the party."

Marco chuckles, "How's that?"

"People really prefer partying to work, Marco."

"I think it'd just be better to do it next week. Say that, say we'll have it next week or something."

And with that the Glaze Event kicked off with the force and terror of a great blind pigeon apocalypse— meteoric ice balls *sprack* and crazily *cack-cack-cack* against the windows, lifting alarmed chins into the air, ears on alert sensing something unnatural and unearthly. Out in the

open office atmosphere employee minimugs rattle
nervously on saucers. The weasel spins his head, his neck,
and his entire body in his swivel chair to face the windows.
"Oh *my*," he said, looking left at Shawn and then right at
Leah, "the Glaze Event has begun." George sprang from
his swivel seat and ran to the window. He jerked his collar
and stretched his neck and pressed his button nose against
the chilly glass and watched his amigos in the parking lot
scramble together. They huddled under their protest signs
and unfurled umbrellas for protection against the icy
onslaught. From his elevated position the weasel watched
them congregate like ants upon a sugary spill. He looked
over at Marco ignoring the hot babe in his office, probably
thinking about fucking her after his big party—a party that
the weasel still hadn't been invited to. Fuck that guy, he
thought, fuck his big head and big hair and big cars and big
house and his big fucking dick. Look at him in there—he
really doesn't give a shit about the 2s. "Baahhk," George
half-shouted. Running his hands stiffly over his head he
thought about all the lives that had been ruined by the
invention that he now represented. He felt like a traitor to
his people, and he got it into his head that his Hispanic
heritage must be the reason he hadn't received the group
email. Well, Jorge decided right then and there that he was
going to turn this party into an all-out fiesta.

The phrase "Fuck you," burst abruptly from under
Marco's office door. Shawn glanced knowingly at Leah.
The weasel turned from the window to see Shawn's
knowing glance. Now *everyone* in the office scanned the
room with wide eyes peeking just above white mugs, the
look of uncertain conclusion following prolonged trench
warfare. Then Lana exited boss's office in a huff and
everyone ducked back into his or her respective trench,
pretending not to have noticed. They scrunched their
bodies so low in front of their Egostatistical screens that
hardly anyone saw Marco dashing for the elevator.

Turning back to the window, Jorge watched as Marco walked into the parking lot.

And seeing Marco, Juan yelled, "*HEY*...for fucking douchebag jes press one, mang."

"Go fuck yourself, Juan," Marco replied. "How're those gloves treatin' ya?"

"I don't need jore stupid gloves," Juan said, and threw one glove at Marco.

"Chyeahhhhh," yelled the other 2s, reacting to the toss, but not following suit.

Marco hears them but can't really see how many protestors are actually in attendance since they remain hidden behind an umbrella wall that does provide shelter against the razor-sharp ice balls skittering across the slick pavement.

"Okay...*please*, listen to me for a second," Marco says. A few eyeballs do peak out between umbrellas. "*De veras, regresen a sus casas y a sus familias y disfruten el fin de semana.*"

Here follows a long, stunned, pause. Whole faces now emerge from behind the umbrella wall as though Marco Salazar has earned the trust of an ancient, hidden civilization. Falling hail immediately punishes those peeking, stinging lips and ears—the oppressor notices flecks of blood on their chapped lips. He feels for them. He wishes he'd thought to bring extra ChapStick. He hopes that his rehearsed line instills in them the anti-Wanda camaraderie he feels.

But instead of union or truce, someone slings an errant ice ball from behind the black umbrella fortress.

"*Hey*," Marco says, watching the thing whiz over his shoulder.

Then Juan Miguel bends down and grabs a ball with his bare hand and fires it directly at Marco's face.

"HEY," Marco yells, easily ducking Juan's weak throw.

The software man bolts toward his car. He covers his ears to protect against both the falling precipitation and the meager projectiles sailing in his direction—he is careful not to slip on the slippery parking lot pavement. He ducks in front of his car, by the warm engine, where the ice is slushier and perfect for crafting superior winter weaponry. The clever boss does not launch right away but instead builds his ammunition, carefully shaping leaden ice/snow balls all around his popping brown oxfords. Pitiful ice chunks fly in his direction, seemingly launched blindly, via catapult, from behind the umbrella wall. Most don't even reach him. Others land harmlessly on his car, which he has started remotely. Juan then dispatches an offensive—his two chief lieutenants emerge from the umbrella confines. They circle cautiously, searching for an angle of attack. But as they try to find exactly where the young software man is hiding a glorious mixed ball is sent skyward. It's the oldest trick in the book: with the two 2s out in the open and distracted, Marco fires another ball that connects with one lieutenant's neck. The defeated adversary clutches his throat and groans, "Ugggg," then lurches back behind the umbrella wall. The second 2 is still circling, and Marco circles too, squatting behind his car to ensure protection against any kind of direct hit. Now resting just below the passenger door, Marco can see his second pursuer through the car windows and knows that he's clueless about Marco's position. Salazar checks to see what the other 2s are doing, but they're huddled together and he can't see. He's pissed that they're using *his* umbrellas and *his* gloves against him. He pops up with a thick ice ball in each hand and fires a laser with his cannon arm. The offensive 2 ducks and narrowly avoids the toss but doesn't expect Marco to be packing two balls at once. When the 2 rises up to return his misshapen answer, Marco lets rip a beautiful strike with his second ball, scoring a face shot. "*OWWWWWWW*," the 2 yells, putting his gloved hand to his face. Marco quickly ducks behind the car and circles around near the hood.

"Hey mang, chill out—that was ice," shouts Juan Miguel.

It's a trick. Marco doesn't respond. The 2s all fling ice chunks toward his former position.

"Hey, *hey look*," says Jorge, "the boss is in an all out war down there." Coworkers rush to the window as the 2s are lobbing their pathetic unformed ice wedges taken straight from the ground. Office spectators grasp the entire situation and clearly see that Marco has already abandoned the area the 2s are targeting. The software man is restocking his ammo by the hood. With all of Egostatistical distracted by the parking lot showdown, the weasel slips back to Shawn's desk. Shawn is an assistant service coordinator without anything to do most days but keep a stern or flustered look on his face and make sure his office email is always open.

"We can't just leave him down there like that," Leah says.

"I'm not going outside in this," replies Shawn.

The collected office breath fogs the window. When Shawn wipes it clean he mentions the chilly glass and speculates that it's probably below zero out there and also confirms that their boss, Marco Salazar, is a straight-up badass—he's not wearing gloves *or* a hat. With slush from his hood, Marco shapes round ice balls and lines them up all along the outer edge of his car from the hood to the driver's side door. The 2s continue to fruitlessly pepper his proximity with piteous pellets. What fools—they grip the ice too tightly, many step with the same foot as their throwing arm, and they are all completely unwilling to remove their gloves in order to form something capable of doing damage.

Marco runs his fingers through his iced locks. He's leaning with his back squat against the car hood. He shakes out like a dog and momentarily warms his hands inside his jacket pockets. His breath perfumes out in front of him as the ice continues to spit down and tap dance viciously on the ground. With his back still turned, Marco takes an ice ball in each hand. He looks at the rest of the balls leading to his driver's door to make sure they're stone-frozen—and they are indeed. Marco rises so slightly from his crouch and spins like that famous Willie Mays play and dispatches a bullet with audible velocity at the middle of the unsuspecting umbrella wall. The first ball lands powerfully and knocks one umbrella holder right on her ass, and in the process reveals an umbrella-less 2 she'd been shielding. Marco takes the second ball, cocks, steps, and drills the now exposed foe on the left shoulder—he spins violently and topples to the ground on top of the señorita with the umbrella. Their moans meet just above the tundra.

"Holy shit," Shawn remarks from above.

Juan Miguel scrambles to form a worthy ball, but he's too late. He's got four injured amigos off to the side whimpering and commiserating about Marco's stinging fastballs—not only do they lack the perseverance necessary to continue, but their cries infect the uninjured with debilitating fear. As Juan ditches his last glove in a desperate effort to fashion a formidable ice ball, he too is struck on the neck, "Arggggg," he complains. Feeling the blunt pain all the way in his jaw, Juan Miguel scurries toward what's left of the umbrella wall. Marco Salazar does not need to throw his remaining three balls to make it into his car. He shifts into reverse, casually, and then into first—he injects his coil lighter into its socket as he pulls out of the Egostatistical parking lot, completely unharmed.

"THIS ISN'T OVER, MANG," Juan yells, rubbing his neck.

Marco doesn't hear that. He's hauling eastbound ass on the expressway. Cars dawdle fitfully forward all around him, like lemmings headed for the edge, taillights lit red alert, wipers sloshing and re-sloshing, arms flung frustratingly into the air, palms pounding steering wheels, honking horns, middle fingers stab the air, torsos loll back and forth in the cars like dead men afloat—there is a flagrant disrespect for rules governing the HOV lane.

The weasel creeps away from Shawn's computer, unnoticed. The rest of the staff is still laughing and pointing by the window. Jorge puts on his jacket and slides his winter cap over his head, then mumbles, "All right, guys, I'm taking off then," and heads for the elevators.

Outside, the 2s attempt to gather themselves after the painful defeat. The relentless jagged precipitation dampens their spirits further—if they try to talk, it stings their lips; if they look up, they're blinded by a thousand needles. Their outfits shine stiff with rime. Their toes are numb. The wounded shiver on the verge of tears.

The weasel ambles out toward his ailing amigos. He shakes Juan Miguel's hand and asks him if he wants to go to a party. Juan Miguel massages his neck and answers that he doesn't really feel in the mood for a party right now, but some other time for sure. But then Jorge informs him that the party is at Marco Salazar's house and Juan changes his mind. Juan tells the gathered mass about this development and they shout "Chyeahhhhh," and hoist their signs and dance a showy revival dance.

9

*B*y the time Mark Salaznek had turned twenty the sweetest thing left for anyone to say about his mother was that the years had been unkind. "Her...*condition*, well, it's deteriorating," was the most common whispered phrase. What Claudia Salaznek really looked like was the aftermath of some torrid flesh mudslide. All her loose skin and nerves flopped and drooped and folded for gravity. She no longer bothered with ashtrays. She lay there, sloped and shitfaced drunk, flicking her Marlboros upon the growing filth pile that was her lap.

Mark had no choice but to remain in the area for college. He took an apartment in the city but only stayed there if he had a girl—he couldn't possibly bring anyone home to Patchogue. He tried to hire live-in nurses to help with Claudia because he couldn't provide the constant care her deteriorating condition required. But he couldn't yet afford to pay the type of salary necessary to convince anyone to deal with her. With a right hand lively as ever, Claudia swung bottles at those approaching to change her diaper. She gurgled incomprehensibly for Mark, "WURZ MY FUGGIN' SUN JASHTUPIT SUGGGUVABISH?"

She blew smoke at them and threw her food on the floor, and she started fires on purpose with whiskey, newspaper, magazines, a lighter and some old mail. The firemen and ambulance would come to take her away and change her clothes and call her son. She enjoyed these things. Neighbors complained to Mark that the constant presence of emergency response vehicles had lowered their property values so he stayed there as much as possible and gave up the apartment and gave up the girls.

Mark commuted two hours each way into the city for his classes. Claudia loved having him around.

"Duneverrr furgit hoooyarrrr," she mumbled, cigarette bobbing in her mouth like a diving board above the drool pool.

Her speech deteriorated further: "Dunver fugit hooarrr," and Mark knew what she was saying but only because that's all she said anymore. She needed help. He needed to *do something*.

"Dunnn fooyarrrrr."

And he started working on a speaking machine.

"Dunn fuyarrr."

"Dunfyarr."

"Dunfarr."

"Dunfrr."

"Dunf."

He plugged it in.

"Mom, press that button."

"**Yes.**"

"Holy shit, it works," Mark answered.

"**Yes.**" She pressed it again.

"Try the other one, Ma."

"**No.**"

"Yes!" Mark said.

"**Yes.**"

"Yes."

And thus began the verbal regeneration of sweet Salack-neck—or, perhaps, the initial step in Claudia's mechanization. Marky skipped down the stairs a few months later in his brand new suit all ready to present his speaking machine to a group of potential investors. To "yes" and "no" he'd added: bathroom, bath, cigarettes, whiskey, food and help. He put a jack in the thing and connected it to the telephone. Though truly, the invention only worked for Mark's phone calls.

"Mom?"

"Yes."

"I'm on my way home from the city. Do you need anything?"

"Yes. Whiskey. Cigarettes."

"No problem. I'll see you soon."

The machine failed in all other cases. Some operators had more patience than others. Here is the most successful outgoing phone call Claudia ever made:

Ring.

"Hello?"

"Yes."

"How may I help you sir... or uhhhh, ma'am?" Clueless about the grammar rules for conversing with machines.

"Yes."

"Yes, Ma'am...Sir? What can I do for you?"

"Help."

"Ma'am this is Bruno's...Bruno's *pizza*."

"Yes. Help. Food."

"Okay, you want food. Do you want pizza?"

"Yes."

"Okayyyy, friend. Do you want pepperoni?"

"No."

"No?"

"No."

"Do you want *any* toppings?"

"Yes."

"Sausage?"

"No."

"You mean *cheese*?"

"Yes. No."

"You want cheese?"

"Yes."

"You want something else too?"

"Yes."

"How about a buffalo chicken pizza? You want that?"

"No. No."

"Guess you *really* don't want that, huh?"

Claudia squirmed with frustration on the couch and kicked her right foot in the air. She knock-knock-knocked the phone against the side of her head.

"Okay, okay, okay, I think I got it...black olives!"

"No."

"Peppers?"

"No."

"I don't know what the hell else there is, friend."

Claudia flicked her cigarette down by her right foot and squashed it out. She collected as much wind as she could; sucking the odious living room air into the polluted depths of her diaphragm she mustered one magical word, "*Fijj*."

"Fish?"

"Yes."

"Ohhh, you want *annn*-chovies?"

"Yes. Yes. Yes."

"People sure do love their anchovies. I don't see it myself. Pickup or delivery?"

"No."

"Delivery?"

"No."

"Okay, pickup?"

"Yes."

Given this less than outstanding record of achievements, it's no surprise that Mark felt nervous going into his meeting—this thing, this invention, he knew, wasn't ready. The fresh suit also gave him jitters. Somehow designers haven't quite mastered the concept of a fit suitable for recent graduates of the adolescent class. A young man like Mark goes into the *men's* store and they give him some shitty black thing with padded shoulders and pleated, *cuffed* pants that just doesn't fit right at all and instantly he looks sixteen again. They send him out of there with a grin so goofy it's wicked and a 'Good luck son' that's more like a kick in the ass or the societal equivalent of slapping an explanatory message on the back of the sucker's new suit: First Big Interview.

To combat the evil fit Mark brought with him the positive daydreamy intentions so characteristic of those his age. When he unplugged the thing from the wall in Patchogue he told Claudia he was going to do good in the world—to give speech to the voiceless. What he was bringing to Manhattan on this day was nothing but the baseline, a simple foundation on which teams of happy employees would build wildly. People that haven't spoken to each other in years without assistance from pen, paper, or sign language would again converse freely. Blessed independences we don't think about like Claudia's pizza order would be granted. Perhaps those who've never spoken at all might learn by using the machine—an adult's first words, a once mute husband or wife tells their spouse, I love you. Severed lines of communication reconnected. Lines that did not and could not exist now established—an entirely inclusive conversing community.

"Dunf," Claudia said, waving Mark out the door.

"Don't worry."

By 8:15 am that Monday the Long Island Railroad car smelled of unflushed piss and sweat and hairspray and soggy newspapers and Redbull and coffee and residue from thick green soaps and smoke and gum (workaday potpourri)—when new groups of passengers crowded into the cars all garbling about the news and holding their Redbulls and coffees and chewing their gum or spraying hairspray, they performed a pained nose-motion and looked accusingly at everyone else. These (other) people sure do stink. Mark pulled his notes out of a knapsack and rehearsed the things he wanted to say. He imagined how the conversation might go. He noticed a babe across the aisle and up a row from his seat and the ever-present male fantasy of an attractive woman alone on public transportation took hold. Mark couldn't turn from the display of gentle dexterity made by her lightly-pinked fingernails breaking her bagel into bird-size bites. At each successive stop the conductor reminded everyone that *this* is a particularly crowded rush hour train and that they're expecting another crowd at the next station. The conductor came down the aisle and punched her ticket, "Thank you," she said in a voice Mark would later describe for his friend Stone—in the description a combination of the words: flower, heaven, sun, and songbird. In Stone's reply, a combination of the words: fuck, man, Jesus, and pussy.

"Good morning, passengers. The conductor would like to remind everyone that this is a particularly busy rush hour train and that those riding together should sit together."

And why wouldn't it be, at 8:45am on a plain Monday? Did they make this announcement every single Monday? Would it be improper to assume that ninety percent of the riders are repeats who ride forty-eight or more Mondays out of the year? Do we make these troublingly obvious announcements to cater to random Monday riders who for whatever reason may not agree or be aware that bodies stacked together in aisles constitute 'particular' busyness? Anyway, no matter what, isn't *everyone* in here riding together?

Mark tried to refocus on his notes—just black blotches scrawled over the page. The dexterous distraction up there might be his unraveling. He could feel sweat collecting in the fabric at his armpits. He removed his big black jacket and put it on a hook. The jacket served as perfect shade against the striking morning sun. She slumped back in her seat so her knee could reach and rest upon the seat ahead. The sun hit her face as she started popping baby carrots into her mouth one...at...a time. The girl looked out the window, thoughtfully, not nodding off or anything—her profile cut like a sparkling starlet against the humdrum towns whizzing by. She rolled up the sleeves of her jean jacket just enough to give her bracelets room to jangle up and down her arm—thin tanned arms, by nature, not that odd salon orange. Mark closed his notes.

"Good morning, passengers. The conductor would like to remind everyone that this is a particularly busy rush hour train and that those riding together should sit together."

Mark leaned across the aisle, "You, uhhh-*know*..." he said. She didn't hear him at first as it was getting quite loud on the train. "You know *what?*" he asked.

"*Me?*" she asked, startled, turning slightly to face him.

"Yeah."

"What?"

"We're actually *all* riding together," Mark told her.

"What?"

"The conductor keeps saying that those riding together should sit together. I mean, aren't we all riding together?"

"I guess," she laughed politely and got up to join Mark. She was a small lady with a full face, almost pudgy in its cheeky roundness and an inviting contrast to the sharp Salaznek brow. Her two radiant silk scarves framed her face, highlighting its dimpled glory. The way she walked across the aisle one could imagine her dancing for a lifetime without a moment of embarrassment. Mark studied the way her black sunglasses sat atop her wavy brown hair and liked the way her eyelashes flashed curiously at his lap. "What's that?" she asked.

"It's a *device*...that I'm, like, inventing—you know?"

"I can't say that I do."

"Right," Mark giggled. "It's for people that can't speak—it's kind of a speaking machine."

"So you're an inventor then?"

"Not really."

She turned her whole body in the seat to face Mark

who'd become aroused by the slight gloss on her lips and the charmingly crooked shape of her teeth. He lived there, in the present, where they were having this conversation, but his mind ran free to a place it'd never been—a metaphysical virgin apple orchard. They ran together in that orchard, he in a wool scarf and she in these same scarves, dancing and singing and kissing below all the ripened apples, oh autumn. And it wasn't simply the proximity of her shocking beauty that affected him—it was what this one represented—that orchard, something more, some...possibility, an abstraction that seemed to transcend her physical form. Something you could easily write off as bullshit your whole life if you never experienced it—these are the little moments that lead to tandem power-walkers and that tender tone of voice couples use to warm each other's hearts, the way it sounds when they say 'baby'. He looked at her and wanted to travel *generally*. He imagined her decorating their home with seasonal soaps and towels. He imagined himself cooking dinner and posing for photos and taking out the garbage on Tuesday night and saying baby every night.

"You know, it never occurred to me that people might need something like that," she said, "probably because I can talk. I love talking. I talk all the time. I think I take talking for granted."

"I made this one for my mom."

"Oh, she can't..."

"She passed away," Mark lied.

"I'm so sorry...ummm."

"It's Marco," he lied again.

"I'm sorry to hear about your mom, Marco."

"Her condition had been deteriorating for a while."

"Well, I'm Melanie."

He shook her hand, bracelets jangled up and down her arm.

"Maybe you can tell me how your big meeting went sometime?"

"I didn't say it was *big* or anything."

"I mean, I just figured...the suit and all."

Mark looked down at his suit and felt uncool, felt that he needed to be something more than himself, felt an urge to lift himself to the height of the presence next to him. Melanie looked really cool. She spoke as if she knew it. She was undoubtedly a chick you'd imagine dating an NHL superstar or some broad-shouldered finance guy. Mark decided that he'd better start working out seriously.

The outcome of Mark's big pitch now meant more than an opportunity to finance around-the-clock care for Claudia. It did mean that, of course, but with that kind of support he could finally move out of Patchogue and maintain his peace of mind—he wouldn't just be leaving her to rot. He'd be a man of the world, his own man, one of the twisted Manhattan bastards bobbing and weaving all around him. Their energy lifted his shoulders and his movement became more stride than walk. He slung his coat over his shoulder and felt the blood in his guts driving him toward the door of the monolithic building. He wanted to be the man in that room. He ran his hand slowly through his hair, with purpose, pulling it to the side and back. He looked passerby in the eyes, glaring below the deep rim of his brow with a new brand of seriousness and confidence—gotta rock this shit out, get that girl, kick these motherfuckers to the curb, fuck him, fuck her, fuck that, be it, be big, be Marco: The Credo of Salazar, get back or get punished.

The comfy fat guys looked and treated him like a young man who had lost his shoulders to a bad jacket, yawning and checking their watches, "Mmmmya, *sure*, Marco, *sure*, we grasp the significance, the...*necessity*...of such a thing, but the demand doesn't seem to be there. I mean, I'm not hearing from these mute people. They seem to be doing just fine with that sign language. You bring up making phone calls, sure, that'd be nice for them. It works well for you and your mother. I can see that. But like you said, there is an issue with outgoing calls. This thing has eight buttons, and that's great, but think about it long term...what if someone else's mother doesn't want *whiskey* and *cigarettes*, just for instance, so you're telling me we have to make *each* device, *on* demand, specific to the *customer*? Either that, or we produce *one* machine with two hundred buttons on it? Then how big will that thing be? You certainly couldn't carry it around with you. It'd be just for making phone calls. We don't see phone calls for people with speech impediments as being *that* important, Marco. I'm sorry, it just seems to me, and I think I speak for my partners when I say this, that unless you can figure out how to attach the damn thing to the person so it can read their thoughts, or whatever, what you have is a nice home-aid device, not something we can market for profit."

After his spanking Marco lit up a smoke and looked at the sky, like twenty-year-olds do after their first foul taste of the world. People still bobbed and weaved all around, and he cursed them for not acknowledging his dreadful existence.

"MARCO!" someone called, a man from the room street-jogging his way.

"Thank God," the man breathed, "you're not on the subway yet."

"Yeah," Marco said, blowing smoke.

"I'm LaMichael Carmichael, nice to meet ya...again." Carmichael took out a cigarette and continued, "You write code, right?"

"Yeah."

"Yeah?"

"*Yeah.* So what?"

"Flip that fucking bitch around, baby."

"What?"

"Listen," Carmichael said, looking at Marco with the swollen undereyes of a committed drinker, "you just put the machine on the other side—boom."

"What?"

"What that idiot Lloyd said about attaching the device to someone's brain... Check it out, you just design the device to understand the phone instead of the person—eliminate the operator, the machine responds to the buttons *already* on the phone."

"Oh shit."

"Oh shit is right, kid. If we can preprogram the questions, then the *machine* responds, press one for this, two for that, three for the other—and on and on. Then from that choice, another set of options—one for movie showings, say, and then the thing reads off the titles. You pick the one you want to see and it reads times for that movie. Two could answer questions about pricing, hours of operations, *whatever*—and bang, it reads *that* shit too. No one will ever have to actually speak to another person over the phone again."

Marco finished smoking with a new opinion of the sky. LaMichael Carmichael quit his job and supported the young software man throughout the process of creating the world's first Automated Answering Service. Despite L. Carmichael's efforts to keep the device free of racial prejudices, the men could not anticipate the havoc that such a machine, once unleashed, might create. The devil began his career as an angel. The world is filled with nasty things and nasty people that started out peachy. You can't ever be sure when, where, why or how you crossed to that other side. And even after you have crossed, aware of the change, you may yet be under the impression that you've made the right decision, the noble choice. But what you really did was fuck up royally. And what we must all understand is that bad feels good and that there's no going back.

10

*M*arco drives through his front gate and slowly up the slick driveway. Fat, bare and ancient oak trees feel the weight of accumulating ice. Limbs bend a dangerous canopy overhead and sparkle like the crystal chandeliers in Marco's mansion. During the summer the *gorgeous* whitewashed brick façade provides an elegant Old World feel. Folks loaf around the property in shorts carrying cocktails. Landscape artists caress fresh blooms, bend to one knee for a sniff. But now the sun's gone bye-bye. The bricks are dull, morose. The sky craves refreshment, unable to remember what it once was, a black chalkboard erased to gray dust after some profound lesson. The mansion sits like an under-stuffed ossuary.

These are the days that meteorologists dream about. Major airtime for Stone DeFoné—townspeople tucked in, tuned in, front and center fella. The lone regional voice tasked with unveiling the intent of an angry regional god. This bitch could get national attention. Tree branches might fall anywhere at anytime—onto power lines, onto cars, onto people, whole trees onto cars with people inside. There were chilling whispers of 'stocking the basement' amongst the elite. The word "crisis" began to circulate around the weather center. Marco Salazar tuned in to watch the afternoon forecast along with the rest of Long Island.

"Wanda, Wanda, *Wanda*," Stone began, walking past the X, face filling the camera—the usual shaking of his head no-no-no, a vein pulsing through his forehead betraying any attempt to look resolute. "She's coming, Long Island. I'm putting a *full* Ice Storm Warning in effect until noon tomorrow. That includes Eastern Nassau, Western Suffolk, Central Suffolk and Eastern Suffolk counties. This lighter purple area *here* indicates only a freezing rain advisory for Central and Western Nassau counties, where residents can expect a lighter glaze. The deeper the purple, the higher the impact of the storm." He indicates the various shades with his finger. "Now, let's break it down in terms of what you can expect for tonight: extremely hazardous travel, especially in Central and Eastern Suffolk Counties. These are areas where you really need to stay off the road. You can expect some tree damage overnight—trees with weak branch junctures, dead or decaying limbs and any fine branching are more susceptible to fracturing as the glaze thickens. Power outages will be scattered. Be patient, Long Island. Some of these outages may last between twelve and twenty-four hours—right now they're just isolated. We'll keep a close eye on that. Now take a look at these *frigid* temperatures: Massapequa: eight. Deer Park: eight. Ronkonkoma: four. And East Quogue an ab-so-*lute*-ly freezing: negative two."

"Oh *my*," announced Umi Culvida.

"Yes Umi, as the devil bestows his wrath with fire, it would only make sense that God uses ice."

"Wrath isn't *bestowed*," said Marco, sensing the pressure put on local writers to uplift Wanda's prestige.

"So, Stone, is that today's fun fact?" Todd Michaels joked.

"Actually, Todd, this isn't going to be *fun*...at all. These current temperatures don't even factor in the wind chill, which will only be increasing throughout the day and into tonight causing temperatures to drop *precipitously*."

"Well, that's certainly bad news for Starbucks," added Umi.

"What?" asked mostly everyone watching the News.

Marco burped some coffee back into his special orange mug that he'd re-stolen from Lana's bag while at work.

"What'd you just say?" Todd Michaels turned and stared at his red-outfitted co-anchor, who now also wore a smile so wide that it hurt your face to look at it.

"Oh, *you* know," was her reply. But Todd didn't know, Stone didn't know, Marco didn't know, nobody knew. Though, in a way, they all had an idea. The wretched terror on Umi's face, the toothy chaos directed at the wrong camera—it was Wanda. Umi Culvida was first to feel that vise grip to which Stone had alluded. The freezing forecast may have frozen her brain. Her intelligence quotient dropped precipitously. With each blink of her maniacal eyelashes she saw nothing but a wash of high-impact deep purple storm warnings. "I ummm, I, ah-haha," she laughed, "ah-haha," blinking, "I gotta go now." And go she did. She picked up her leather bag from under the desk, slung it over her shoulder and lobstered away from the newscast. One camera operator with a sense of humor followed her first few steps before some director with no sense of humor cut to commercial.

Marco moves from the kitchen into the rest of his hollow home. The thickening sheet of ice clutches the roof above him and sounds like a noose as it's tightened. He drifts toward the vaulted living room, really lingering, hoping that maybe the longer it takes him to get there the better chance he has of finding someone. No such luck. Stone's voice calls from the kitchen television, "Baldwin, Bellmore, Bethpage..." but is interrupted by the unmistakable CLAP of a giant tree limb snapping outside—the rupture so thick and unavoidably real that it rattles Marco's spine, chokes his breath, he shivers. The resulting bareboned echo reverberates against the windowpanes and calls attention to the abnormally vacant streets. "Garden City, Hempstead, Hewlett..." Salazar moves to the French doors that lead from his living room to the patio. His breathtaking property was built on a hilltop to "ensure fantastic views of the estate's lands." This is what the real estate agent had told them, wearing a tailored suit and sounding as though he'd fashioned the hilltop, designed the house and constructed it. Though what he really did was sign up for some classes, pass a test or two and get a piece paper that entitled him to a generous percentage of the sale for pointing out updated kitchen appliances, walnut flooring and new double-glazed windows—things he also had no part in designing or building. Things the genius young software man and his fiancé could certainly appreciate on their own. Melanie stood at the French doors and gasped, "Look at *that*," referring to the views of the lands. Marco remembered feeling uncomfortable about a place this big for the two of them. The realtor insisted that they'd have a family soon enough, and given their age, income and occupation they'd probably want some room for entertaining guests, and just look at that pool, that pool house, the guest cottage—it's absolute opulence, Mr. Salazar, it's luxurious, sophisticated, you can *pamper* all your friends and loved ones. "Island Park, Lawrence, Mineola..." Melanie slid her fingers through Marco's. This got to him every time. It felt different, even better, holding hands with her ring there. She looked at him with oozing eyes soaked in the possibility of a future so bright. She squeezed his hand, and the realtor felt butterflies in his stomach—the rush of a potential sale. He stood a polite and comforting distance behind Marco. He also looked into Melanie's eyes. He observed the tight handholding and knew, in this familiar moment, that it was best to be quiet and wait—to let them ponder the view. "Okay," Marco said. And as Melanie chirped yay-yay-yay, leapt, teared and turned to embrace her fiancé, the realtor, Richard Listit Clayton Orenstein Jr., clenched his fists, eyelids, and bent his knees in that silent *yesssss* of the extremely lucky. It's probably true, Marco thought, that such mansions might never sell if not for dedicated realtors: "New Hyde Park, North Lynbrook, North Valley Stream."

Ice dominated today's fantastic view from patio all the way down the hilltop. Marco felt the heavy chill coming off the glass, attacking his feet from beneath the doorframe. Distant trees looked like black cutouts, empty forms of alien shape serving an uncertain purpose in the otherwise white world. The sound of splintering timber became commonplace and formed a strange rhythm with the odd inventory of towns logged in the background, "North Woodmere, Oceanside..." by a forgotten voice from Marco's past echoing reminders of what? Better days? "Oceanside, Old Bethpage..." Stone called to the people who could hear nothing but the sound of trees collapsing, listing them in groups like dead regiments. A solemn memorial, a reminder to those fortunate enough to still be alive, "Old Brookville."

"Ohhh *no*... No, no, no, no, no."

Oh, yes.

Gone, everything—down, off. The television snapped silent making way for the defeated sigh of the just unplugged or powered down—a supposedly sweet relief. Lights butted out and the powerful bright white of the exterior world poured through the mansion's every orifice.

11

*T*he Boom Boom Latin Lounge of Jersey City, NJ is five blocks from the Egostatistical offices—windowless, Dijon yellow stucco, solid baselines pound the walls of three-story residential buildings on either side. This isn't a place tourists would enter on a whim. If a tourist did enter on a whim, perhaps compelled by the inviting palm tree logo on both awning and swinging neon sign, he or she wouldn't stay too long. This is a place for schemers. Sideways glances with bizarre scowls efficiently promote the opinion that almost no one is welcome here.

For local schemers there is delicious sangria made fresh daily, a jukebox, billiards table and out back a gazebo for intimate cigarette breaks. Jorge leads the 2s into the lounge where they immediately shake the ice from their hair and shiver and brush wildly at their stiff crusted clothing. They add to the giant puddle at the entryway before moving to the bar.

"What the hell happened to you all?" asks Gabriela, the wonderfully full-figured barmaid.

"Nothing, just pour a few bottles of the sangria," replies Jorge.

"You want a few *carafes*, Jorge?"

"Si, *carafes*."

The Latin Lounge staff calls Jorge "pinhead" or "*chorlito*" behind his back. He's always so damn rude to them, plus his head really is tiny—it's a bothersome combo. It's just that no matter how badly he would like to fuck Gabriela (and he would, he thinks about it almost every night), he knows he never will. It frustrates the hell out of him. Yet he comes in for happy hour every day after work to take the edge off before the long railroad ride back to East Quogue. This situation might also be considered a bothersome combo. Gabriela tells her coworkers that when Jorge stays for a fifth drink he develops a proclivity for staring at her fingernails whenever she shakes the cocktail shaker. She estimates he's left his address and phone number on over forty receipts without ever mentioning it the following day.

The two bloody lieutenants start snatching bar napkins five at a time. One dabs at his lips, the other rubs his neck and asks for ice.

"Hey...hey...*HEY*!" Gabriela yells at them. "You want some paper towels? Go to the bathroom and clean up, *por favor.*"

Unsure what to do the two men look at Juan Miguel who does indeed confirm that they should clean up in the *baño*. He nods in that direction and they go, leaving a few bloody bar napkins behind for Gabriela.

"Come on, Jorge, just tell me what happened," Gabriela says.

Juan jumps in, "We got in an ice fight with Marco Salazar."

"*Really*?" she laughs and pours the carafes. "The sexy software guy?"

"No, the fucking racist asshole," Jorge snaps.

"I see him around the neighborhood sometimes. He's nice to me...I think he's cute."

The weasel's face is reddening, yes, Juan can see it.

"That's probably jes because you're so beautiful, hunny," Juan says.

"Maybe he's just nice."

"Fuck that," the *chorlito* shouts. "The guy never even wanted to include número dos for Español. What about *that*, Gabriela?"

"People forget a lot of things, Jorge. Mostly everyone speaks enough English to understand it anyway. Didn't you say you work for him?"

"Yes."

"And what were *you* doing there? You work there too?" she asked Juan Miguel.

"We were protesting."

"Still? I thought you gave that up months ago."

"We want to be number one. Number two is racist. He's taking a shit on our community. Don't you even care that his invention put all of *them*," he references the crowd of 2s glowing by the jukebox, "out of work?"

"I mean, yeah, I guess so." She serves the drinks and goes to answer the phone, pickup order—no doubt. Juan watches Jorge watch her butt. All the other 2s come over, most of them still rubbing their hands together for warmth. Given this frigid situation sangria would seem an unusual choice, but you gotta be yourself, stick to your guns, dance with the girl that brought ya and drink traditional cocktails.

"So how are we gonna get this bastard?" Juan asks. "There's no way to drive in this...even if we did have cars. Do you at least know where he lives?"

"I didn't get a chance to write down the address, people were around. But don't worry, I have a plan."

"Oh, a *plan*..." Juan displays an aggressive set of air quotations. "You have a plan to get twenty people to a party we're not invited to and don't know the address of in the middle of a fucking ice storm?"

"Wanda."

"What?"

"The storm's name is Wanda—kinda like your name."

"That's nothing like my name, mang. That's a girl's name"

"Sure it is. Juan...Juan-*duh*, see?"

"*Excellente*. What's that have to do with the plan?"

"The News."

Juan turns slowly to face Jorge. Juan's fist is balled up below the bar. He thinks he could probably punch it right through the weasel's head. "If you keep being so obtuse, I'm going to punch my fist through your head."

"Well, that certainly is direct," Jorge replies. "GABBY," he calls, but she's on the phone *and* writing down an order. "GABBY," he tries again anyway.

"Just gimme a minute and I'll show you the plan. I need her to change the channel."

The two men wait for Gabriela to finish taking the order. They shake their shoulders to the salsa music hopping from the jukebox. The song has a feverish clapping rhythm, always building, all percussion and piano, "Chyeah, chyeah baby, I could party to this one," Juan says. "For sure," replies Jorge, bouncing his pinhead from shoulder to shoulder. The 2s dance in circles behind them. The soggy lane between bar and restaurant area is clogged with shaking hips and snapping fingers. Their bodies have a unique relationship with the music, bonded to the beat. Someone shouts, "¡*CALIENTE*!" Unable to resist another moment, Jorge and Juan get up to join them. Jorge's head bounces from one shoulder to the other like a supercharged metronome. The scuffed wooden floor is streaked with salt stains and plastered with napkins—the barback called in, scared of Wanda's wrath. The 2s come together to cheers in the jukebox's neon glow, in the spirit of the great palm tree, "Welcome to the party," Juan shouts over the tune and nods his head to the jukebox DJ. When the music is over the entire crew takes part in what they call The Sangria Slam. All the glasses and carafes collide in the air, "AYAY-YAYAYAAAA." Gabriela applauds. Sangria surges from the glasses onto their clothes and spills all over the floor. They laugh at this—it's part of the camaraderie. The countless red blotches dissolve bits of the salt-stained ground giving the impression of a hundred tiny murders outlined in chalk.

"Okay, let's get down to business," Jorge announces.

"Yeah, what's the plan?"

"Gabriela, please, turn on News Ten."

"Why do you always want to watch that crazy Long Island guy?"

"Gabriela, *please...*"

She does it.

"Gabriela, the sound..."

She does that too.

All four Boom Boom Latin Lounge TVs flash to an image of Todd Michaels sitting next to a distractingly empty chair. It is now quite clear that Todd has a fantastic tan: "Authorities are on the lookout tonight for a man who they say received a massage from a woman at a Massapequa hotel, told her he was a cop and then raped her." The screen shows a video of a man wearing a hat labeled "P" walking up a set of stairs in what just might be a parking garage—or the hotel itself. "And now, more from the weather center and News Ten Meteorologist Stone DeFoné."

"Why are we watching this shit?" Gabriela asks.

"Just wait," replies the weasel.

"Wow, Todd, real scary video there. For those of you watching this, consider yourselves lucky to have power. There are *massive* outages all across the island. Wind gusts of up to forty miles per hour, Cascade Failure likely in densely populated areas—it's too dangerous to send Skytracker out there. This storm system Wanda will be one—"

"Stone?" Todd Michaels cuts in, finger to his earpiece.

"Yeah, Todd? What?"

"Stone, we have a caller on the News Ten hotline...it's

about your father."

"Put 'em through?"

Camera cuts back to Todd, very tan, earpiece—whispering to producer loud enough so the audience can hear: "Can we do it? Yeah? Yeah. Okay."

"You're on the air with News Ten Meteorologist Stone DeFoné."

"Hello?" says the caller, his voice echoing awkwardly throughout the studio.

"Yes, hello, you're *live*," Stone says.

"Hey man, hey *Stone*, you were right...it's us, it's the guys you met outside Tanked yesterday. You were right." The caller's voice trembles, he's outside again, the sound of wind is devastating to the TV viewing audience.

In the background of the call, echoing through the studio: "Holy *SHIT* dude, are we on the air?"

"Yes, I remember you. Now please remember you're live."

"Dude, you were so right...this storm is nasty. My jeans are like, totally frozen stiff," the caller laughs.

"Dude, are you on the *air*? Let me talk."

"No, get outta here—*I'm* gonna tell him."

"Tell me what?" asks Stone.

"Dude, your dad's a fucking hero out here right now."

"Please caller, tell me what you mean."

"Okay, so he's here in Patchogue. No one can drive. It's nuts, just like you said, roads like ice skating rinks. But your pops, he's shuttling like, tons of people from the train station back to their houses. He's taking people to and from the bar—they're cheering him on, people are partying on the bus. He really seems to be enjoying himself."

Juan turns on his stool to face Jorge.

"Bingo," Jorge says.

Stone approaches the camera, closer than ever before. Lounge TVs show only eyes, nose, mouth. "Caller," he says, tilting his head down, more serious, "*caller*...you must get my father off the road. Wanda will continue well into the afternoon tomorrow. This is going to be worse than Helga. Do you understand me?"

"Dude, what's he saying? Let me talk."

"Shut up. He says it's gonna get worse. Okay, Stone, we'll try. People aren't gonna like it very much though. Get *away* man, I'm talking to him."

"Just let me say one thing, please. Stone, hey *STONE*... STOOOOOOOOOONE, can you hear me?" The second guy screams into the wind. Stone and Todd recoil, the shrieking studio reverb like a dog whistle delivered directly into the eardrum and the unfunny director mercifully cuts the call.

"I think we better hurry up," Juan says.

The weasel shouts "*Vamanos*," and waves his arm at the group of 2s, still a bit stunned by the live broadcast.

"Where are you going?" asks Gabriela.

"To a party," replies Señor Pinhead, "at your boyfriend's house."

Gabriela perks up: "Can I come?"

"Don't you have to work?"

"You're the only ones here. I'd rather party."

"Jes let her come," Juan Miguel says.

"I'll bring the sangria," Gabriela adds.

"Fine."

Gabriela bends at the knees one, two, three times. Her breasts follow the knees in tantalizing hot waves as she claps her little tan hands together in celebration. The weasel takes note of her sexy fuchsia nail polish. The 2s suit up by the door. They put on their jackets and gloves and hats and pull their heavy hoods over the hats. Zippers zip-zip-zip like gangs of bundled-up school children rushing home for the holidays. They grab their umbrellas and protest signs and march out the door.

12

*I*t didn't take long for Wanda's chilly breath to invade Salazar Palace. In any crisis level storm the rules and routines of normal life no longer apply. Marco skipped his shake, said fuck the workout and uncorked another bottle of the Biondi. It didn't warm him, but the plum tint and powerful nose brought a hopeful disposition. When the power goes out it is imperative to take immediate inventory of your candle collection—if your belly is full, light is the first thing you will need to survive. Marco Salazar has a dynamic candle collection. It is his constant gift—birthdays, Christmas, Easter, Columbus Day—you name it. The common phrase, "What do you get a guy who has everything," is really overused on him. Somehow the answer is always: A Candle. It's just like, hunny, they have an entire cellar filled with wine and liquor from Europe, we can't just give them a bottle of Cab-Sav—it's embarrassing. Oh, a plant? You want to give Marco and Melanie a *plant*? No. No way. Remember last summer? They had those little dudes running all over the estate tending to goddamn acres of plants. You're seriously not considering giving them a calendar, are you? Oh, my God, no way. Headphones? You're joking...*head*-phones, for the hottest young software man on the planet? That's probably the stupidest thing I've ever heard anyone say. Come on, let's just get them a candle. It's heavy. It smells good.

First, Marco unpacked the Wild Sea Grass: delightful. Put that bitch right on the kitchen island, center of everything—fitting, sea grass, there on the island. In the fresh light he swigged straight from the bottle of Biondi then opened the Angel's Wings: fancy, with a triple wick, heavy, good smelling: a true blessing. Irish Trio came next, must drink to that. Into the living room he brought Blue Summer Sky, Beach Flowers, Bahama Breeze, Beach Wood, and Berrylicious. The French doors served as portal to and from countless pool parties and barbecues. Surrounding floor-to-ceiling windows once allowed abundant light—these candles belonged there.

Into the study/library Marco delivered the Autumn Leaves, laid them on the large ovular table at the center of the room. Here they'd spend fall nights reading—when the sun went down way before dinner time, too dark for a tandem jog, too cold for a swim, not yet cold enough to head north for skiing. The only season with two names, you just can't trust it for anything. Marco placed the Girl Scout Coconut Caramel Stripes by Melanie's micro fiber Millsap chair. She'd always be snacking on something, slurping her coffee too loudly while Marco tried to read. With her staticky hair sprawled out behind her she'd chew and talk and laugh and say, "Wait...listen...listen to this sentence." Marco would agree, great sentence, and she'd ask, "Oh, am I bahhhhhh-thering you or something?" with a wicked grin on her face that he could never grow tired of or get mad at.

In the expansive foyer he placed the Bay Leaf Wreath, and in the dining room went Bavarian Pretzel, Candy Cane Lane, Early Sunrise and Drift Away. And now, sure, Marco could see, but he quickly understood why people use the phrase 'candle light,' instead of just saying light. The longest indoor shadows possible enveloped the house, shading a blurry black aspect over everything once bright and familiar.

Trees and limbs continued to split and crack and pop from all directions with the rhythm and consistency of a demon pulse. Salazar expected the words "Fee, Fie, Foe, Fum" to come thundering from his yard any second now. He wandered back to the French doors and saw groups of limbs lying eerily about the ground, misshapen and freakish, like a looming errand. As the world seemed to crumble and encroach upon his solitude the young software man came face to face with the possibility of reading a book to pass the time, by candlelight. Unimaginable. My toes are cold, he thought, and so waddled slowly on frozen feet into the foyer and up the grand staircase. The wind pressed stiffly against the whitewashed brick façade. Marco could almost feel it on his face—the barrier separating the interior and exterior world began to wear thin.

Marco put the bottle of Biondi on top of his dresser and rifled through a disastrously unmatched sock drawer, desperate for warm toes. He'd never realized the demand of owning so many socks until he started doing his own laundry a few months back. The showy work socks, like the ones on his feet, were easy to spot in the diminishing light—he haphazardly flung these to the ground and persisted on his quest for a certain pair of wool boys. "Come on, come on, come on," he mumbled into the darkness, multi-colored patterned socks flying over his shoulder like a thief on a tight schedule. "Eureka." There they were; fuzzy, warm, thick, gray—functional. He sat on the edge of the bed, happily wiggling his toes, admiring how they moved when thawed, joyous inside the new wool residence. He walked into his closet and flicked on the light switch—obviously no juice, must be the wine. Takes time and sobriety to free ourselves from default settings. Absolutely no natural light could reach this interior chamber. Salazar fumbled with the Biondi and plunked it on what he thought was the central dresser, which housed watches and other jewelry—a showcase. He turned to the eye level row of closets behind him. He ran his fingers along the respective fabrics, searching for something itchy and dry in the absolute darkness. He wanted his fingers to stick to the material but instead his tips kept gliding down the sleeves of rich foreign materials—closet after closet after closet. No wool to be felt. A beefy bellowing gathered at the bottom of Marco's driveway. He heard it humming with speed for a hundred yards below the bent frozen oaks, unleashed like a starving ghost shark. His chill and lack of wool the wintry equivalent of blood in the water. The gust came to feast on the front door, blasting the entire house with the wretched unending shriek of a million unpracticed trumpets.

"Oh, *ouch*," Marco shivered, pulling his body together. And yet the great gust persisted, snapping thick branches like twigs at an accelerated rate. The young software man couldn't fold his arms tight enough to protect against the blistering advance. He pawed at his clothes quicker and quicker. No...no, none of them were right. Wanda had him surrounded. With the whole damn mansion in her grip she squeezed, blowing and blowing and blowing, dominating Marco's mind until finally something exploded—a thunderous crunch. A crisis level smash heard only during natural disasters. The potent detonation of force from the prolonged howl, like a cannonball fired into a warehouse full of bones.

Marco's eyes opened wide and his body shot perpendicular. "What...the fuck...was *that*?" The wind quit. Silence again. His hand landed on something heavy, he grabbed it. Hell, he needed to get back downstairs. His wools socks bounced back down the grand staircase. He flung the large polyester coat over his body as he sprinted for the French doors, anxious to see about all that commotion. *Shit...* The three-bedroom guest cottage, once ideal for entertaining guests, cozy and sophisticated, now split down the middle, crushed and agape like a victim. Worst of all, this latest catastrophe had all the makings of another serious errand—perhaps, even a full-blown project. What an ass-kicking bitch, this Wanda. "Fuck you," Marco told her, gulping his wine. "Fuck...*you*," he stuttered into the glass doors, extending consonants in the grand tradition of drunkkkks everywhere.

Unable to stand the carnage any longer, Salazar moved to the spacefridge. His belly bubbled and begged for something more substantial than grapes. "Okay, let's see," he said. Opening the sleek metal door he discovered nothing, supreme vacancy, no meats, no cheeses, a lot of useless sauces and dressings—naked shelves. Marco reached into his pocket with a mean scowl on his face, pulled out a device with visible aggression and started thumbjabbing at his dietician.

Chew. Yo Chew.

Marcooooo. What is up my man?

Get your ass over here. I'm starving. What are you doing?

Marco you're crazy, I'm not going anywhere in this.

Chew tomorrow is the first. Come on. I don't have anything to eat.

Marco I sent you a message last night to see if you needed me.

What?

I told you this thing was gonna get bad.

Come over. Tomorrow's the first.

It's leap year-tomorrow is the twenty-ninth.

What the fuck?

Marco I told you all this yesterday but you never got back to me so I figured you were good. I know you've been going out to eat a lot more lately.

My phone was broken.

Shit. I'm sorry. I don't have power Marco I think my phone is gonna die.

Chew just come over, please. Cook me something, we can party. I'll open the Rioja 92.

This last message hung in the air.

Chew? The Rioja?

Nothing. Chew's phone had died, just like that. Salazar thumbjabbed his device a little more then put it to his ear.

"Hello, you have reached the Long Island Power Authority. *Para Español oprima número dos*...For billing inquiries, press or say one. For trouble with your service, or to report an outage, press or say three."

"Three."

"Sorry. I didn't get that. For billing inquiries, press or say one. For trouble with your service, or to report an outage, press or say three."

Marco pressed three.

"Thanks. We are currently experiencing unusually high call volume. All of our customer service representatives are busy at the moment. The approximate wait time to speak to a customer service representative is forty-five minutes."

Wildly inappropriate Muzak streamed from the device. You'd imagine the title of this so-called song to be something like "Honeymoon Hotel." Marco had to thumb the button that ended the call. It was just too much to bear.

He picked up the Wild Sea Grass and went into the basement. He tiptoed around all the broken glass and whirled down the steps to the cellar. He pulled bottle after bottle, showing each label to the Wild Sea Grass, searching for the '92 Rioja. When finally, his device buzzed. Chew on his way...Melanie? Lana. Yes, Lana. Beautiful Lana, self-starter, extreme attention to detail, ability to multi-task, feels comfortable working individually or with a team, darling Lana, great organizational skills, thrives in the fast-paced, pressure-packed environment.

Hey, I didn't get to send the party cancellation email out until later in the afternoon—I hope no one showed up.

Not yet.

Okay good. We were all so distracted by your ice fight.

You like that?

Not really. I was still kind of pissed at you. The 2s are going to be REALLY pissed at you.

We were just having fun.

It didn't seem like they were having fun.

Come over.

Are you drunk?

I'm hungry.

Where's Chew?

He said he's not coming over because it's leap year.

That and maybe because the roads are like sheer ice Marco.

Just come over. I'm in the cellar. I have a candle-it's like ancient Rome.

You ARE drunk!

Yes I am. And I need your assistance.

You want my assistance?

Badly, I'm powerless.

Good one. Why don't you start boxing up Melanie's stuff like I asked you to? You don't need power for that.

I might.

Marco my phone is about to die. Call me in the morning okay?

Just come over.

Again, no reply. Another device by the wayside. Another message in message purgatory. The flame of Wild Sea Grass flickered from a Salazarian sigh. How long must this desolation last? A hundred circular shadows stared from the wall but said nothing. Blank deadwide witch eyes looming in the crisp cold basement—hello, my pretty.

"Fuck *this*," Marco decided. He grabbed a non-Rioja, some cardboard boxes and went upstairs.

"Hello, you have reached the Long Island Power Authority. *Para Español oprima número dos*...For billing inquiries, press or say one. For trouble with your service, or to report an outage, press or say three."

"Three."

"We're sorry, but your response was not understood. For billing inquiries, press or say one. For trouble with your service, or to report an outage, press or say three."

"FUCK YOU. ZERO. OPERATOR. OP! UH! RAY! TORE! GIVE ME A HUMAN BEING,

GODDAMMIT."

"We're sorry, but your response was not understood. For billing inquiries, press or say one. For trouble with your service, or to report an outage, press or say three."

Marco thumbed the three.

"Thanks. We are currently experiencing unusually high call volume. All of our customer service representatives are busy at the moment. The approximate wait time to speak to a customer service representative is one hour and thirty minutes."

The absurdly inappropriate, mind-numbing, sunny psych-ward Muzak came bopping gently through the device. So sweet, just tumbling along like butterscotch biscuits and fresh squeezed OJ. It pitter-pattered into the world like a virgin in pleated khakis. Could this tune possibly last for an hour and a half? No human being should be subjected to this level of antagonism. This must be the shit that inspires clowns to run up daycare murder sprees. Marco knew, absolutely, that there would have to be a Monday meeting about this on-hold Muzak. And no, a conference call wouldn't do.

The chilly young software man ended the call. He had a feeling the few living customer service representatives were told to stay home. These are moneymaking days for cell-service providers. It's not like the power authority didn't already know about the outages. It's also not like they had any clue when power would be restored. People don't want to hear, "As soon as we can sir—we're trying our best ma'am," from some asshole getting paid and not doing the actual work. In uncertain times the truly desperate will spend hours on hold waiting to get angry at the vague answers they know are coming.

Marco noted his battery percentage like a heart rate: barely functioning on fifteen percent. His breathing turned a little uneven as exhaustion, hunger and drunkenness began to take hold. Without thinking about it he buttoned his jacket. He pulled the vast lapels together over his chest to fight the chill. What *is* this nasty fabric? He felt how it hung, slumped, with militant shoulders. The sleeves brushed tragically against his knuckles. He felt like a child and he knew—his first suit. "GROSS," Marco shouted, and the word ricocheted back in his face from the vaulted living room. He pulled the lapels apart. The lone button popped and fell innocently to the floor. He balled and twisted the suit in his hands with all the drunken force of an extremely unsatisfied customer. He shoved the suit into one of the cardboard boxes and charged into the living room. He picked up one framed photo and pushed it onto the suit, hoping to squish it down more. Another frame went on top of that. The hot software man pushed his bare palm into the box one and two and three times, shoving harder with each successive thrust. The glass gave way and a slicing sensation cut the middle of his palm, which only made him angrier. That big stupid coat, "Good," he said, "great," he picked up a sleeve and wiped blood on it and laughed. The living room scent was so waxy and muddled it felt like he was choking on flowers. Marco shoved everything he could into the first box and then crushed it down with a few wicked woolen foot stomps—it looked like he wanted the coat to just disappear. Maybe he wanted all of it to disappear. And surely it would when Melanie came to retrieve it, or when the sanitation professionals did. But all that shit, all the stuff in those boxes—it's really only just *stuff*. What a word. Perfect for describing all that might go into a box or any number of items left behind. Would a catalogue of sun-drenched moments be preferable here? A bit of nostalgia? Do you believe that's what makes any twosome so special—a plentiful reserve of photos and trinkets from weddings and ballgames and holidays and vacations and parties of the same people showing the same pose in various stages of tan? Do you imagine that when Marco Salazar thinks about Melanie every single day of his life he meditates on commemorative seashells? Nah—that's all stuff. Actual memories are no more static than the people who fill them. They get stored not in a cardboard box but within the most complex human organ. They are free to move about and their appearance shifts in the ever-changing light of time, going, going, gone. Good riddance to the big black jacket. Fuck it. It's a keepsake; some things we can outgrow—no matter the size. But some things we can't let go. Some stuff gets *ingrained.* Some of it's good, no matter who comes to take these boxes, and no matter what disposal methods are employed, there's no erasing all that sexy barefooted dancing from the software man's memory. But some of the other ingrained stuff is bad. These bad things always weigh more. It's the bad that defines who we are, and negativity now dominates the day.

Marco brought the boxes into the garage. He needed a smoke. He called Lana and left a message: "I'm done. Come over if you get this." The moon taunted him from the small garage windows, calm and silent, one-eyed. It hid behind twisted black branches that, given the icy thickness, did actually appear glazed—they tentacled into complex spirals, fusing with the yellow moon a lunar design resembling some bad tattoo. The familiar racket of ice thrashing against ice no longer filled the void left by all that forced powering down. The constant, unchanging, uniform static created a pandemonium out of silence. Wanda had such a tight squeeze on Marco that he felt claustrophobic. He needed to leave, now. There's no noise here, no action, nothing—his whole life switched off like a snowy analog TV. The black and white dots specked his vision. His ears were cemented by white noise. It was freezing in the garage. *He* was freezing in the garage. But he needed a cigarette after all that packing. When he looked down through the lighter's flame Marco found his answer, his escape: the briefest flickering image of a recent dinner party with Melanie's friends Sara and Steve smiling so wide on top of all the other stuff. "We come out here to unwind every now and then. Whenever the city gets too crazy, you know?" Steve had said.

"Welcome to Oheka Castle, Long Island's premier hotel and estate. For directions press one. For weddings, events, or corporate sales, press two. For group hotel sales, press three. For fine dining, press four. For mansion tours, press five. For media inquiries, press six..."

"Un-*fucking*-real," Marco pleaded.

"For the corporate office, press seven. For a hotel reservation, press zero."

He pressed zero.

"Oheka Castle. This is Suzanne."

"Oh? Yes...hello?"

"Good evening, sir?"

"You have power?"

"Yes, we do, sir. Is there something I can help you with?"

"I need a room, please."

"I'd be happy to check our availability for you, sir." Marco heard her punching a keyboard behind the insufferable spongy oral sound of her gum chewing. "All we have left is the Olmsted Suite," she reported.

"Book it."

"Sir?"

"Yeah?"

"Sir, I should tell you that the Olmsted Suite is twelve hundred dollars a night."

"It's no problem." Marco's chuckle is relief, not conceit—maybe a *hint* of conceit.

"Fantastic, sir. This exceptional suite pays tribute to the Olmsted Brothers who designed the reflective and stately formal gardens here at Oheka Castle. You will have access to two glorious balconies that overlook the great lawn and reflecting pools. Of course, I do apologize, but the reflective pools are frozen at the moment."

"That's fine, Su..."

"*Zanne.*"

"Suzanne. Don't worry about the reflective pools. You

really saved my life."

"Feel free to check in at anytime, sir. There are plenty of other people staying tonight. Executive Chef Horatio Ettore Felice has decided to conduct an impromptu tasting for tonight's guests."

"That sounds wonderful. Really, thank you so much, Suzanne."

"Can I just have your name, sir?"

"Marco Salazar."

"Well then, Mr. Salazar, we hope to see you shortly. I take it you live nearby? The roads are extremely dangerous this evening."

"I do. I've uhhh, I've been there before. Not *alone*, but, well, yeah..."

"Very good, Mr. Salazar. See you soon."

Marco squashed his cigarette out on the cement floor, ran into the house and skipped up the spiral staircase two steps at a time.

13

"News Ten hotline."

"Hello?"

"Go ahead."

"Yeah, I'm just calling in to report a sighting of that crazy bus driver. The weatherman's dad, I guess."

"Mmmhmmm."

"He's haulin' ass down the expressway back toward Patchogue. I figure he's on his way to the train station 'cause the bus is empty. Maybe someone wants to get over there and stop him while he's waiting for the next group?"

"I'll pass that information along as soon as I can, caller. Thanks so much."

"News Ten hotline."

"Hiya. I just stopped by the train station to pick up my wife from work..."

"Mmmhmmm."

"Well, the weatherman's dad is out here. My wife said he keeps opening his doors and asking people where they're going. He asks them if they need a ride."

"Hello, and thank you for calling the News Ten hotline. All of our customer service representatives are busy at the moment but you can leave your tip at the beep."

(Beep).

"Yeah, hi. I just saw a shitload of cuh-razy looking Mexicans get on that bus the weatherman was talking about. They were all carrying signs and yelling 'fiesta'."

"Hello, and thank you for calling the News Ten hotline. All of our customer service representatives are busy at the moment but you can leave your tip at the beep."

(Beep).

"Jesus, what kind of hotline is this? Hunny...hey hunny, you believe this shit? I called the *hot*-line and got an answering machine. Here's a tip: hire some fucking people to answer your phone, okay? Anyway, a whole squad of Hispanics just hopped on that bus you seemed so interested in finding *yesterday*. Thought I'd let you know. Not sure where they're going..."

"Hello, and thank you for calling the News Ten hotline. All of our customer service representatives are busy at the moment but you can leave your tip at the beep."

(Beep).

"Heyuhhhh, I'm down here at the Patchogue L-I-R-R station. That bus just loaded up with Spanish people. Is there a reward involved here? They were all drinking."

"Hello, and thank you for calling the News Ten hotline. All of our customer service representatives are busy at the moment but you can leave your tip at the beep."

(Beep).

"Hi, my name is Julia Edwards and I'm calling to report a sighting of that bus Mr. DeFoné was talking about during this morning's First Warning Forecast...I saw it leaving the Patchogue train station. I think it was filled with Latin American people."

"Hello, and thank you for calling the News Ten hotline. All of our customer service representatives are busy at the moment but you can leave your tip at the beep."

(Beep).

"Yo, waddup News Ten? Just saw that wild maniac

driving a bus full of Latinos out of the Patchogue L-I-R-R. They were hanging out the windows and shit. It looked awesome. Tell that weatherman his dad's a badass. Okay cool, thanks. This is Frankie Minahan. I love your station. Keep up the great work."

14

*W*ell shit, if you told that dweeb Mark Salaznek, or any other man on the planet, that the first day he ever fucked two different women would be the worst of his life he wouldn't believe you. At the very least he'd want to take a shot at it and let the chips fall where they may, as the saying goes.

"*Marco,*" Melanie whispered him awake. Impossible to be certain that Melanie had designed the master suite to feel like heaven, but it did. An all white Elysium—natural light funneled through the sparkling new windows. Silk curtains posed on the hip like anorexic supermodels waiting for the slightest breeze to blow them bare. Delicious glass vases housed flowers that took in the light—ghost orchids and white roses and magnolias, tulips and chrysanthemums, water lilies wading on either side of the bed. Their white sheets absorbed this bouquet and smelled like uninhabited earth—free from toil and surely untouched by sorrow, as the saying goes.

The Greek goddess climbed on top of him and let her hair hood the morning's first kiss. Marco could just barely hear the spacebrew bubbling over all the morning birds chirping outside. They looked into each other's eyes, the way hot young couples do. That dank lascivious look of equal parts love and lust—if you first come across this look as a witness, instead of a participant, you will discover the true meaning of insignificance. Someone said, "Baby," someone answered with, "Baby." What sweet love. Marco followed her smooth movement with both palms upon the wondrous rump. She dug her nails just hard enough into his protein-infused pectorals. Melanie sat straight up now, and Marco moved his hands to her hips. He suggested a slightly faster motion and she abided. The light hit her stomach—soft, flat, tan but natural and not muscular. Her toes curled under her ass as she ran her fingers through her hair. Melanie moaned, "Mmmm, yes...yes...*yes*" and bit her lip just as Marco flipped her onto her back and took over. He slid back in gently and worked at the pace of love, with open eyes, in the morning light. A few thick locks curled over Marco's right eye. Melanie tucked them behind his ear. Sweat beaded on her forehead, he could also feel it behind her knee. He ran his damp hand back and forth along her thigh, squeezing the hot calm flesh he pressed in further and faster. Melanie screamed softly, "Ah...Ahh...*Ahhh*" and pulled him down for a serious kiss. She bit his bottom lip a little between gentle moans, and the blazing hot software man knew then his time was running short. He tried to hold out, ah, just a few, few, few more, ah, ah, oh my god, baby.

After a minute or so of heavy breathing and reflection, Marco asked, "So, what's on today's menu?"

"Well, at ten I'm going to look at a few dresses."

"Yeah?"

"I probably won't pick one today. I have to be back here by noon to meet a *wedding* singer," she laughed. Marco watched her tits shake, a little.

"We're not having a wedding singer."

"*Someone* has to sing."

"Dude."

"Don't dude me. I'm just keeping our options open—I'm going to check out another band after that, and then after *that* meet the pastry chef."

"You're crazy."

"It's *fun*. We're going to have the best wedding ever—I'm pretty sure of it."

"I would never doubt you," Marco said, getting up from the bed.

"What about you, big boss man? What's your day like?"

"Just dealing with more shit from those assholes in my parking lot."

"I think you have to give up that word shit. It's really gotten you in a lot of trouble."

"If LaMichael could have just kept his mouth shut none of this would have happened."

"I know...but he didn't. So you have to deal with it—just keep being sweet to them. It'll blow over."

"I hope you're right."

"I am. I'm always right. When are you coming home?"

"As soon as possible, baby."

The black ride slashed down the expressway. The summer sun put an incredible shining glaze on the car—high-quality midnight paint reflected the surrounding scene as clearly as a lake, trees and signs and lights and cars spit quickly, zinging unnaturally from hood to fender to door then dust. Marco pushed a sweet set of mirrored aviator frames up his nose and smoked out the window. His head naturally followed the rhythm of rock n roll as he steered and shifted with the confidence of any man after such an esteemed pelvic pump. Pedestrian drivers were not as pleased (or awed) by the car's performance at such a speed, which was nearly shocking at that early hour. Marco's movements were so outrageous, in fact, that many commuters watched him flying by and thought to themselves, "Now there's a man who just made love—that *bastard*."

Marco made it to the Patchogue exit in like eight

minutes. He cut over three lanes and ripped around the bending off-ramp, tires squealing a slight protest. Patchogue? What? I thought he was going to work. Not yet. The young software man had one interview to conduct before heading to Egostatistical.

The black car growled awkwardly along the quiet and narrow neighborhood streets. It moved slowly, threateningly, out of place like a black jungle cat in a church parking lot. You might be thinking that bitch is lurking like a black *panther*. But black panthers are usually just some melanistic variant—the opposite of albinism. In America, what you'd see as a black panther is actually most likely a jaguar. And if for some reason you're in Asia or Africa at the moment, staring at what you believe to be a black panther, you're probably staring at a leopard instead.

Marco parked behind a dusty old Civic with bald tires and no sunroof. The car had been red, once, before the sun faded it to something more orange. The orange door swung open and a shapely leg landed on the ground. Salazar opened his door as well and stepped out just as a beautiful Hispanic babe came from the Civic. She pivoted to watch him get out of the car. She took a drag from a cigarette. "That your car?"

"Yeah," Marco answered, walking over to shake the girl's hand. She looked like she'd just stepped off some Caribbean beach, holy shit—tits out to here in a deep white V-neck that made her tan all the more spectacular. She had that effortless sexy vibe, cutoff jean shorts, open-toed flats, like this is more or less how she always looks. And what's even left to say about big brown eyes anymore? Welcoming, enchanting and cute with eyelashes fluttering about, her hair pulled back in a ponytail. "It's fucking hot out," she said, smoking, hoping that the smartass software man would stop staring and invite her inside.

"Come inside," he said.

He led her up and around a fresh wooden wheelchair

ramp and into the house. The girl got nervous at the precipice and held her breath. She felt tremendous relief to discover that the little house had been professionally cleaned and updated: all hardwood flooring, presumably for the wheelchair, along with a new couch, recliner and big fat television with sound. There was even one of those magical chair escalators that allow the disabled to negotiate interior stairways.

"Sit wherever," Marco instructed. "You want something to drink?"

"Is this like, a *test*?"

"No," Marco laughed, moving his fingers through his hair, "you could have a non-alcoholic drink. Water or something..."

"Are you having an alcoholic drink?"

"Yeah, I'll do one, just to calm the nerves," he said.

"Okay, I'll have one too," she said, still standing.

Salazar came back with two cocktails: "Margaritas," he announced, handing her one, "it being so hot out and all."

"Yeah, and morning still...kinda."

Marco sat on the couch. He incorrectly assumed that the girl would take the recliner. She sat next to him, not *right* next to him, not on the middle cushion, but on the other side—close enough to wake the butterflies, you might say.

"So," he began, "you're in nursing school..."

"I'm at VEEB."

"What's that?"

"It stands for Vocational Education and Extension Board. I'm not really sure what the *board* part is all about." As she spoke she stared right at Marco. He watched her sip the first morning Margarita like a real lady, never gulping but enjoying it.

"Where's that?"

"It's in Hicksville."

"Oh, good, so close by."

"Yeah, pretty close—I don't start classes again until fall,

and then only two days a week, at night."

"Do you have any experience caring for disabled senior citizens? Are you studying stuff like that?"

"You don't remember me, do you?" she asked.

"What?"

"Lucia...you know?"

"Lucia," Marco repeated.

"I knew you when you were just Mark Salaznek."

"That was a long time ago."

"Well, I was at that party you had that one time? When Stone beat the shit out of those guys for wrecking your house."

It came to him. The cute Colombian girl.

"I gotta say...I really like what you've done with the place. It must've taken a lot of work."

"Thanks, *Lucia*. I do remember you."

"Listen, I'm really, really sorry about everything. The way we treated you. I didn't know anything back then." She moved to the middle cushion. "I was thinking about it like all day yesterday and wondering if you'd remember me and be all pissed off and mean."

"It's cool. I'm over it." Marco took a good sip, looked down her shirt.

"Then I was thinking, like, I saw you on the News—I kind of read up on you, I'll admit it. You looked good, by the way. You *look* good, I mean."

"Thanks."

"Sure, so, it's just like that. The News, it's like the way all those people think you're some racist asshole, right? Just because of one little thing. It's so stupid. Like, *I* know you aren't. You like me, don't you? And I'm Hispanic." She sipped, moved a little closer. "Sometimes we just make small little mistakes that don't mean anything."

"Trust me, I totally agree with you."

"So how *is* your Mom?"

"It all depends on how you look at it. Intel sent me this wild chair for her to use—it's all electronics, brand new stuff. You'll see it, probably. She still has good movement in the right side of her body. So they put this little touchpad there..."

"Yeah?"

"The pad has a word prediction algorithm programmed into it that reads the movements of her face and throat."

"Right."

"She selects the word she wants. She actually speaks really well now, which is great. I mean, she doesn't speak at all—she communicates, the *machine* communicates, but it has a feminine voice."

"That's great, isn't it?"

"Yeah... She still drinks all the time. I don't think she's happy, which is understandable. I think she's also pissed that I don't come around too much."

"Why did the last girl quit?"

"She got tired of Claudia's smoking. And being asked the same questions all the time... obviously you don't mind the smoking too much. That's why I put it in the job description—and if you get tired of the questions you can just go home, that's why I wanted someone from the neighborhood."

"I don't wanna go home."

"How come?"

"It's embarrassing but...I still live at my mom's. I mean, once I finish the program, I'll get my own place. She's always up my ass about moving out. I'm like, shit Ma, I'm only twenty-two, what the fuck? You know? It's just kind of our culture I guess. Graduate high school, get a job, get married and get on with it. Dealing with Claudia will probably be a piece of cake compared to the shit I get from *my* mom. This is kind of perfect for me actually, getting paid to live somewhere else."

"It's great to hear you say that. I usually feel like I'm begging people to take the job."

"Not me."

"So you want it?"

"*Yes*, I want it."

"Okay, good."

"Is that it?"

"Pretty much. I'll get all your info and set up your pay as we go. I have a *human resources* department now that does payroll and whatnot."

"Where's Claudia now?"

"Oh, shit, right. Boyle, ummm, you know, Stone's dad...he picks her up for physical therapy in the morning."

"Really? That's so cute. On the bus?"

"Yep."

"How does he manage that? Like, how does he get her on the bus and everything? Do I have to help?"

"Nope. She controls the chair with her little joystick, and the bus is handicap accessible now. It's got this elevator thing that comes down from the back and picks her up."

"That's sick. How did Boyle get that thing? He's not really even a school bus driver anymore, is he?"

"Not exactly."

"Did *you* buy it for him?" She took a sip, peaking above the rim with the big eyes.

"Yeah."

"Jesus, you're like *such* a good guy. You have great hair, too," Lucia said, putting her fingers in Marco's hair. "And you're kind of jacked now," she said, grabbing Marco's arm.

"Thanks," he said, cleverly setting his drink down to make way for Lucia on his lap. He wanted that shirt off. She straddled him on the couch and got into some sensual kissing, hitting the neck, the ear, she put her arms up allowing the shirt to come off. Salazar felt like a real stud. He squeezed her ass under the shorts, and he squeezed hard, thinking of what Lucia thought about him the last time they were in this room.

"You know what I want?" she asked.

"What?"

"I want to ride in your car. We shouldn't do this here."

"Okay."

Lucia got right down to business in the car. A real self-starter, Marco wondered if she'd feel comfortable in a group setting.

"Holy fuck, Lucia," he said, shifting.

"Take me to your house," she commanded.

The words 'we definitely can't go there' flashed instantly through the software man's brain, but he was caught in a spell—this type of thing doesn't happen everyday. He thought back to his morning, "Dresses at ten...back here by noon." He couldn't quite see the dash. "Hold on for one second," he said.

"Something wrong?" Lucia asked.

It was ten forty-five. "No, *nothing's* wrong. Keep going. That feels so fucking good."

The mansions of Old Brookville kicked past, blowing marijuana wafts into the black ride. This is how I fucking do it, Marco thought, pants by his knees. Mmmm, that's right, motherfucker—you work for me now. He turned into his driveway, shifted into second and rammed the accelerator. Lucia looked up, "Is this it?"

"Yeah."

"Holy shit," she said, "it's so nice...and freaking *huge*," looking back and forth at the whitewashed façade.

Not bad for a dude with shit all over the floor, eh? He put his pants all the way to the ground and pulled the clutch. None of Melanie's cars were around. Marco hopped over to Lucia's side of the car. He kissed her hard on the mouth, took her shirt off again and pulled the lever that sent her seat back horizontal. Salazar flipped the cute Colombian onto her stomach and pulled off her shorts. No underwear, perfect. She unhooked her bra while he got going. "Fuck me," she said, climbing to all fours, her hands on the headrest that was now in the backseat. She stared out the back window at Marco's house. He had a knee on the seat and a foot where feet are supposed to go—he was giving her the full Salazar, pumping Salaznek vengeance one deep thrust after another.

"Ah, ah, ah, ah," she said.

"Call me Marco," he said.

"Ah, ah, *ah*...oh my God, oh my fucking God, *Marco*...fuck me Marco, fuck me. Ah, ah, ah. That's it, fucking give it to me, ah, ah, ah."

It went on just like that for a while longer. When they were done Lucia asked if she could go inside but Marco didn't want to take any chances, this wasn't nearly worth losing Melanie over. He promised Lucia he'd give her a tour some other time. Of course he wanted to fuck her again. Who wouldn't? When he dropped the cute Colombian back at her car in Patchogue he asked, "So, you like, actually *drive* that car? It's kinda gross, isn't it?"

15

You probably won't be surprised to learn that Marco Salazar has a delightful shower voice—especially when in the grip of a solid red wine buzz. He's not a talented vocalist, exactly, but he has a whole lot of passion—for singing, and showering, and particularly singing in the shower. Give a listen: "Walk along the riverrrrrr, sweet lullaby, it just keeps on flowing, it don't worry about where it's going, ohhh nooo no. Don't fly mister bluebird I'm just walkin' down the road, early morning suuuunshine tells me all I need to know..." Marco strums his air acoustic, appropriately. His pick hand simultaneously soaps his abs while strumming. The master bath shower pummels him with eighteen showerheads. His favorite is the one that shoots up from below. And so this makes for some bubbly sounding vocals, maybe like baby's first song, but the software man is a voracious rocker so you can actually hear him and see the spit flying despite the intense volume of water spouting in all directions. He grabs the air mic in his left hand and puts it to his face, bending his knees romantically as he continues, "You're my blue sky you're my sunny day. Lord you know it makes me high when you turn your love my way," he ponders the ceiling, eyes open, before bringing it home, "turn your love my *wayyyyyyy* yeahh."

Marco shaved by the light of Booty Parlor. He held the candle right next to his face, just inches from the mirror, to make sure he hadn't missed any spots—check. He put the Booty Parlor back on the sink. Leather and Lace, Exotic Woods and Sexy Cinnamon lit Marco's closet with tasteful radiance and smelled of outdoor dominatrix sessions with a hard-working pastry chef. He threw his arms into a shirt, blue-patterned like the tablecloth from any paradise picnic and rehearsed for a mirror. "Yeah, I'm in The Olmsted Suite." Salazar took a moment to admire the line and his abs before buttoning the shirt, "Would you like to join me for some champagne, in The Olmsted Suite? Oh, you would?" He tried his best to sound surprised. "Yes, I have a stunning view of all the frozen ponds from my two *glorious* balconies..." That was it—cute, witty, humble, just doing some jokes. Marco knew playtime would end quickly once he started laying down the all-night Salazar.

And just like that (sweet melody, fresh shave) the software man's thoughts turned to the future. The cardboard boxes, relics of some ancient past, buried and forgotten in the garage. Marco was about to fuck somebody, *tonight*. He remembered what it was like the last time he rolled into Oheka Castle with Melanie and her friends Sara and Steve. Chicks were coming up to the table all night. Freaking dudes were coming up to the table. Marco, you're a Long Island legend, man. Saw you on the News, Marco; you looked *great*. Don't worry about those 2s, Marco; you're a genius. I saw the new crib in *Better Homes & Gardens* dude, sick—so sick. Can I just grab a quick pic with you guys? L-I is behind you, Marco. *We* know you're not racist. Is this your wife? Daaaaaaaamn. Fiancé, actually. Congratulations, you two look *great* together. Would you mind if we just grab a quick picture with you...future Mr. and Mrs. Salazar? Even Chef Felice stopped by the table. Sara was all like, "Was *that* the guy from Taco Highway and Restaurant Wizard?" Yeah, he's catering our wedding, Melanie had replied proudly. Melanie would later voice a small complaint on the ride home about the way Sara stared at Marco after Chef Felice came by.

Mr. Salazar pressed a tie up against his shirt. It matched, but looked a little desperate—like he planned everything, like he really cared about looking good. The Olmsted Suite should be enough—a dude with The Olmsted Suite doesn't need to be wearing a tie. Marco flipped on an understated Cartier tank watch with brown leather band that he thought would do well to define his fiscal position. He blew out the candles and tucked the tie into his pocket. That way, if all the other guys were wearing them, he wouldn't be underdressed

Next, Marco stuffed some potential brunch attire into an overnight bag. The brunch attire doubled as padding for two bottles of Dom Perignon—wouldn't want to bring anyone back to a dry room, of course. Maybe he'd be able to throw a full-blown bash in his suite, complete with drinking, drugs, sex and music—powerful craziness, societal rules thrown out the door in honor of Wanda. Other hot young people drinking themselves dizzy and just fucking all over The Olmsted Suite—a real rock n roll shindig, great hard bodies, asses pumping through the air, stark-naked Salazar just hosing everyone down with Dom while swinging from the goddamn ceiling.

Yes, the software man fluttered down the grand staircase now, blowing out candles in the dining room, in the library, floating into the living room not giving a damn about the crippled guest cottage. He blew away each candle, goodbye to you, and to you, and to you, and to you—issuing carbon dioxide kisses to every precious flame that whispered goodnight and thank you kindly but I no longer need you.

It's almost impossible to imagine, but Salazar got even more excited when he opened the door to his garage and realized he would need to unleash the sickening steel savage, the brute black barbarian—Wanda's Glaze Event marked the first time in the history of the world that Marco's Ford F-350 pickup truck could even be *considered* "necessary." The chrome twenty-twos sparkled in the dull gray garage. This thing could not be driven in the sun for fear that the giant metallic plates would blind all the stunned onlookers. The truck rolled out on six tires—the posterior featured twin sets of dual wheels that allow for hobbies like towing whale carcasses around town. The tires were so fresh that the garage smelled like a rubber factory. The truck's front grill looked pissed, like it needed to run someone over, its metal mouth wide, hideous and indestructible—it had four giant fog lights for gums. The black paint had been buffed in anticipation of winter and it glistened in that wealthy way—the shine of unnamable yet evident superiority, something you just *know* when you see it, special and rare, how the less fortunate feel right before their first limousine ride. When Marco brought the truck home Melanie had looked it over and said, "That looks like you want to take over a small village." Yeah *that*, or cut through this ice storm like it's nothing.

Marco threw his overnight bag onto the passenger seat and asked the steel savage, "You ready to tear this motherfucker wide open or what?" He turned the ignition and the beast snorted to life, huffing fire from twin exhaust pipes and grunting severely beneath the hood. The software man hopped down from the truck and walked to the wall where the garage door openers were all lined up— six of 'em, he pressed the one labeled: "Beast." But nothing happened. No power, no electricity—"Mother-*fucker*," Marco called out to the garage. He pressed wildly at all five other doors and smiled that, oh God kind of terrified smile that acknowledges 'hmmmm I might just be fucked here'. He jumped back into the beast and tried the button on the visor that opens and closes the garage door—nope, just sad desperate click-click-click-clicking, no electronic reaction whatsoever.

Marco ran all ten of his fingers through his slick black locks and quietly said, "No fucking way," to the truck's ceiling. He lit a cigarette and pondered his disastrous predicament. The heat coming out of the vents inside the truck felt pretty good—he'd been chilly for so long now that he'd forgotten the joys of warmth. A little rock n roll kicked through the speakers but Salazar shut it off—this was no time for jamming out. How could anyone even think about rock n roll at a time like this, stuck inside all alone with no one at all to party with.

"That's fucking it." He got down, took one last drag and squished his cigarette out on the concrete. Marco removed his dinner jacket and flung it into the truck. He rolled up the sleeves of his beautiful shirt and stared at the garage door. Fuck it, he unbuttoned the whole shirt and flung it into the truck too. With no shirt to speak of the young hot software man looked at his own garage door with the unspeakable disdain of a mortal enemy. This dead door was the only thing standing between Marco Salazar and a champagne-fueled Olmsted Suite orgy.

He approached the door and saw that it was taller than him, and weighed more.

He did not care.

He stood face to face with the door and puffed out his pectorals, attempting to intimidate the door, but it held its ground.

He stretched his arms and his back and his legs for the door. Showing the door that he meant business.

The door did not care.

"Okay," Marco said.

He bent over and grabbed the door's handle with both hands. Wanda's numbing presence caused entire colonies of goose bumps to rise from Marco's skin.

The young software man pulled that handle with an

oppressed fury. He strained from the root, his feet, to his squatting legs—he squeezed with his hands and wrenched his back and biceps to dangerous levels of tension.

The garage door would not concede a single inch.

He stood up and gathered himself for a few deep breaths. The goose bumps gave way to alcoholic beads of cold sweat. Marco's heart pounded its objection to the sudden exertion and his pulse could be seen beating through the vein at his temple. He kicked the door and yelled, "FUCK YOU." He kicked it one more time, silently, and bent back down for the handle.

Again Marco tugged at the handle with all his might—even more might than before. He jerked and contorted his reddening face to aid the struggle. He pulled and pulled and *pulled*, an anthropoidal screech of pressure erupted from the deep recesses of his body, from the biological dungeon known only as guts. Wine red spittle dripped onto his chin and some flew through his teeth. Sharp ripples of skin cut into his cheeks and his eyes oozed liquid pressure. He opened his mouth, "AHHHHHHHHHHH," and his neck turned translucent with veins like a hundred anguished snakes.

Marco realized Wanda had her vise grip on the door. He stood up and bashed into it with his shoulder hoping to shake it free from the imprisoning ice. He bashed it and kicked it and kicked it and bashed it again. He bent for the handle and *pulllllled*. Nothing. "FUCK YEWWWWWWW," yelled the software man, still tugging the giant door. He pulled and shouldered simultaneously...if I can just shake it free, he thought. Marco's movements took the rhythm of a successful crew team—one-two-three, one-two-three, pull up and shoulder out, pull up and shoulder out, he went, "HUH, HUH, HUH," jerking up with the hands, and then "AHH, AHH," crashing out with the shoulder until he felt nearly sober. The software man worked so hard that his heeled shoes left *signs of a struggle* all over the concrete floor.

This is the exact moment when an unhelpful person looking on might coolly mention, "Umm, I don't think that's going to work." And the hopeless, sweaty, red-faced individual doing everything would reply, after five or six dramatic and heavy breaths, "Well," more breathing here, "what the fuck do *you* think we should do?"

Then the other person, just standing there, will say something annoyingly obvious that, unless you're dumb as all hell, you probably checked three times before you started the wildly physical exertion, like, "Did you even check to make sure it's un-*locked*?"

The pissed off person will reply in the rhetorical here, "Waddaya think I am, a fucking idiot?" And the conversation will drift away because both parties know that if another pointless word is uttered the guy with his shirt off might have an extreme reaction.

"I'm so done with this shit," Marco said to himself.

He looked at the door and told it, "Now you're fucked."

But the door did not care.

"I bet you think this is hilarious, don't you?" he asked the door.

The door did silently agree.

"We'll see about that." Salazar hopped back inside the steel savage. With the truck still in park he pressed the accelerator way down and checked the rearview. Smoke bellowed from the exhaust pipes and plastered the door— a cool gray manifestation of the engine's wicked snarling.

"How about that? You like that?" The entire garage filled with smoke, "You want some of this shit?" Marco asked, "Huh?"

He slowly shifted the beast into reverse.

The door did not care.

"All right," he said. Marco fixed his gaze on the door, by way of the rearview. He pulled his hair back behind his right ear and turned up some rock n roll—go time. In the mirror his eyes looked much wider than usual, his face less hawkish. This is good, he thought, as he absolutely hammered the accelerator—rubber tires erupted, the software man's bare body shot forward into the steering wheel before the truck's ass collided with the garage door causing an equatorial split, but no release. Marco violently slammed back against his seat and pressed the accelerator to the floor. The truck and door stood deadlocked, tires burned into the concrete and released a prolonged deafening squeal through the cracked door and out into the terrible night. "Come onnnnnnn," Marco urged the machine onward. The RPM needle lived in the red danger zone. Marco pushed and pushed his back into the seat in a pathetic attempt to gain momentum. The garage door started to give way. The crack got wider and allowed gusts of Wanda's chilly precipitation into the garage. As the truck's rear caught its first peak of the winter wonderland, Marco felt assured of imminent freedom. He turned up the music and went all-toe to the tip of the accelerator, pressing so hard his butt rose from the seat. Salazar showed no regard, no concern what-so-ever for the welfare of his garage door as it finally split. Searing white light filled the garage. The rear dual-tires rolled up and over the bottom half of the door. "AAAHHHHHHH HAHA, FUCK *YEWWW*," Marco yelled, laughing like a cruel maniac, a deviant homeowner on the run.

But lo, the software man's jamboree ended after about two joyous seconds. The back of the truck did make it out, sure, but the bottom of the garage door stood planted, rock-solid in ice, and held the truck aloft so that it looked like a teeter-totter—with Marco Salazar as the "weighty" end on the ground. He still held down the accelerator but quickly realized that if he were to gain reverse traction, the upended vehicle would only flop forward over its nose and possibly crush him to death.

Marco turned off the ignition, grabbed his clothes and jumped out of the vehicle. Sadly, or perhaps thankfully, the elevated end of the seesaw stayed in place.

Now just when you're at your lowest, right when you've realized with near certainty that the task at hand is impossible, *this* is when the fool's errand foreman will strike again. They will suggest some other, even more ridiculous strategy for solving the problem like, "Why don't you just go outside and break up all the ice *first*...and *then* try to pull the door open?"

Yes. That's not bad. Not bad at all, Marco thought. He took one last look through the garage before heading inside to put on his winter clothes. He gave the door the middle finger, and said, "This isn't over yet," but the door laughed—an all white laugh, giant white ice-teeth glimmering in victory. But Marco saw the black beast as a missing tooth in that grin—a tooth that *he* knocked out.

16

"*H*ello, and thank you for calling the News Ten hotline. All of our customer service representatives are busy at the moment but you can leave your tip at the beep."

(Beep).

"Hello? Uhhhh, Hello? *YO*, is anybody there?"

"Dude, what's going on? Let me talk."

"Shut up. I'm tryin' ta drive. Hello? *Hell*-ooo? I think they hung up..."

"Hello, and thank you for calling the News Ten hotline. All of our customer service representatives are busy at the moment but you can leave your tip at the beep."

(Beep).

"Shit, I got it. Oh. Stone, hey Stone...it's us again. The guys you met at Tanked last night. Just wanted to let you know we're following the bus."

"What's he sayin'?"

"I told you to shut the fuck up, Charles...it's a goddamn machine. I'm leaving a message. Sorry about that, Stone. Yeah, so anyway, we're out here following the bus. He's driving around this shitty little neighborhood. I'm not sure what's going on. Those foreigners are hanging out the windows with signs. We've seen them launch a few bottles out too. The bus is shaking back and forth but your dad's driving it pretty good, I gotta say. I'm not having as good a go of it. We've had a few, if you know what I mean, pal. This bitch Wanda's got everybody down..."

"Gimme the fucking phone already."

Rumbling static noise here, indeterminable utterances...

"Yeah, that's what I *thought*." (Heavy breathing) "Stone...it's me...Charles. We're gonna get him off that bus. Don't worry. I promise you. I'm gonna do it—I'll do it for you. What are we talking about for a reward here? Nahhhh just kidding buddy. No, seriously, call us back at five five five five, five five five five."

"Hello, and thank you for calling the News Ten hotline. All of our customer service representatives are busy at the moment but you can leave your tip at the beep."

(Beep).

"Hi. This is Cheryl Seymore over on Powers Street in Patchawwwwgue? Wanted to report a sighting of the bus that your weatherman was talking about—it's parked on my street. And actually, its headlights are shining right into our house. Could you just please send someone over here to get rid of it? Sorry to bother you with this, but the cops said they're not coming out for a light complaint. Thanks so much."

"Hello, and thank you for calling the News Ten hotline. All of our customer service representatives are busy at the moment but you can leave your tip at the beep."

(Beep).

"Karen Sears here. What's with you people not answering your phone—what if this were an emergency? Maybe it *is* an emergency, actually, for all I know. Anyway, that *bus* Mr. DeFoné mentioned on yesterday's First Warning Forecast is parked across the street from my house and the engine is rumbling something terrible. My boy is complaining he can't sleep. There's a lot of people in-*side* the bus hooting and hollering and carrying on, and

I'm pretty sure they're drunk, just so you know. And they sound foreign. Normally I wouldn't care, but a handicapped woman lives there and the bus doesn't usually come around until morning. Seems fishy is all."

"Hello, and thank you for calling the News Ten hotline. All of our customer service representatives are busy at the moment but you can leave your tip at the beep."

(Beep).

"Mmmm-*hi*, this is Patricia Etheridge of fifteen Powers Street in Patchogue. I'm calling to voice a complaint for disorderly conduct? The authorities just like, *completely* ignored me, and this involves that bus your weatherman was talking about on yesterday's First Warning Forecast. Well, I'll tell you, it's basically full of South Americans. I was just out for a run and all of a sudden they were yelling and screaming from the bus windows and inviting me to some *fiesta* or something. It really was very rude. Someone should get over here and do something about this. I think one of them said something about my body."

"Hello, and thank you for calling the News Ten hotline. All of our customer service representatives are busy at the moment but you can leave your tip at the beep."

(Beep).

"Hey, Meteorologist DeFoné...just got your message. Jim Hurricane Schwartz here. Don't even mention it, pal, it's no problem—I'm on the scene. Got the tires all chained up. I'll track him down for you. You just keep it cool in the weather center—the people need you. This storm system is no joke and your coverage has made me proud. *Schwartz*—over and out."

"Hello, and thank you for calling the News Ten hotline. All of our customer service representatives are busy at the moment but you can leave your tip at the beep."

(Beep).

"Stone, it's Charles again. Listen man, I'm on the bus now and I gotta just say these amigos are pretty fucking cool..."

Raucous laughter, enthusiastic bilingual shouts of joy.

"So, uhhhh, yeah, I think we're just gonna hang out and party with 'em. You should come. There's like hot chiiiicks...sangriaaaa...it's *warm* in here, everything man."

17

Sweet Lucia lasted a solid month before she'd had enough. The early mornings were *her* time—she'd perform hot yoga exercises in her bedroom, make coffee, have a smoke, study elderly nursing trends, check energetic morning television and nearly forget about the impending onslaught. Then, like clockwork, the magical side-stair escalator would click to life. The cute Colombian cringed. It came down so slow and steady. The torturous buzzzzzzzzzz that brought the old lady to the foyer gave Lucia the feeling of watching the last few sandy pebbles of life bleed into the bottom of an hourglass.

The chair would again click into place at its terminal destination. The unmoving old woman sat staring into the living room at Lucia. The caretaker stared back, at that face, the left side slipping away like a pizza delivery that fell off the seat. Lucia's face looked more like something from the dessert menu—foamy cappuccino with a cinnamon finish. This daily standoff could last minutes before Claudia started wailing, "HOOA FUGZ MARGO SALLZERRR?" Lucia thought that maybe if she ignored Claudia long enough she might just elevate right back upstairs—that upward buzz goodnight, as the face finally disappeared behind the wall, was the best moment of Lucia's day. If she waited too long, the right-handed banging commenced, "CUMMANNNN GITME, CUMMANNNN GITME, CUMMANNNN GITME." And some goddamn days that nutcase Boyle DeFoné would randomly resume his old bus route and forget about Claudia's therapy—and so Lucia would get stuck with her the entire...fucking...day. The banging, the smoking, the drinking, the bathing, the piss and shit and vomit— sometimes Claudia passed out downstairs in her chair and Lucia had to wheel her into the foyer, lift her into the magical chair, walk up the stairs, lift her out of the magical chair into the classic non-electronic upstairs chair, and from that chair load her into bed, peel the soiled clothes off, deal with that ripe funk and then go to sleep all alone just praying Marco Salazar might pay her his weekly visit that made it almost worthwhile.

But Marco's visits only got more sporadic, and Boyle's penchant for driving his old bus route increased exponentially as summer came to a close. Lucia spent more and more time with Claudia Salaznek, even developed a taste for Claudia's (now) fine whiskey. The two women staggered through their days sedated, in various and often impressive stages of intoxication. Lucia would nod off by the tub and wake up to Claudia's wet fingers groping her tits. Claudia would fall short of landing in the magic chair and tumble down the stairs, into the door—thud. Lucia had other guys over to the house. Claudia asked if she could watch one time. Lucia let her watch one time.

The girls threw a weird party—an end of summer shindig. That old bastard Dick Salaznek showed up and after harassing Lucia moved on to his ex-wife, who would allow it if he could solve the puzzle. Dick loaded his princess into her magical chair escalator and followed her upstairs. He picked her up. Her skin folded upon his as he carried her over the threshold like their sunlit honeymoon of yore. The old bastard set her down on the bed and lifted the red party dress that Lucia had picked out for her, he slid his conductor pants to his knees—he was just drunk and desperate enough to overcome the foul odor. He whispered in her ear, "I'm sorry, I'm sorry, I'm sorry," as he went to work. All the noises were terrible, squishy, apprehensive. Dick kissed the wrong side of her face and laughed. Claudia grabbed an alarm clock with her right hand and smashed him with it twice before he could wrestle it away. He flipped her over and stopped feeling sorry. Claudia moaned and drooled into her pillow. Dick turned her face so only the good side showed—his dear wife, freckled and orange, all aboard.

The Salaznek's shared a cigarette afterward. Claudia could not quite speak but the two did communicate. A lone unanswerable question volleyed as silently as the cigarette between them. That third person, their son, who used to live in this place...he's fading from them like smoke as it rises.

The conveyer clicked to life later than usual the morning after the party. Claudia had the form of a successful electroshock patient—her hair projected *out*, twisted and stiff like many orange lightning bolts. She wore her drool like a trophy. The strap of her red dress slept in the crease of her elbow as she sat there half-smiling at Lucia.

"Well look at *you*," Lucia said, helping her into the Intel chair.

"**Let us go...outside...and have a...cigarette.**"

Lucia followed the joysticking, motorized woman out onto the porch. She felt bizarre, the incongruous relationship between Claudia's appearance and the computer's sick clean grammar almost too much to bear in these jittery hungover hours.

Healthy sets of neighbors flew by the porch, not looking. They dressed in athletic apparel and spoke in the familiar elevated speech of those out seizing the day, judging slumped smokers and heavy brunchers—the debate over who missed the party, and what that party entails, could escalate to war on days like this. Not everybody loves the sun. Little blackbirds pecked at the ground and dipped between twigs. Children on skateboards and bicycles wheeled down the street screaming nonsensically, parents after them averting helmeted heads from the smoky porch scoundrels.

"Fucking *hot* out," Lucia noted.

"Yes...it is. I am fairly certain...that this is what...they mean...by...Indian Summer."

"Your ex and his buddies stole your whiskey, ya know."

"Wham...bam...thank you...ma'am."

"Do you think he's gonna call?"

Each question required Claudia to hold her cigarette in her mouth while jabbing the monitor. The resulting speech made Claudia Salaznek appear to be the world's greatest living ventriloquist.

"I would not mind...so much...if I never saw that...jerk...ever again."

"Well, was it fun?"

"I can't feel...anything."

"That sucks. I'm sorry."

"I guess we are...going to need some...whiskey."

"I'll go in a minute."

"Can I ask you a favor...low sea you?"

"Sure."

"It is a...hot day. I would like to go to the fish market...it is in...Old Brookville."

"I know the place."

"I used to have...bar bee cues...here with my son on...hot days."

"Yeah," Lucia looked longingly out to the street.

"Do you like him...my son?"

"Everybody likes your son."

"Where is he?"

"You don't know?"

"No."

"You haven't been to his house?"

"Does he live in...the city? He used to love...the city."

"He lives by the damn fish market. Right in that neighborhood."

Lucia noticed a physical reaction to this piece of information. Claudia's whole right side perked up. She gurgled to the point of laughter and slapped her hand on the armrest several times.

"Mark used to stare...at...those mansions...every Monday."

"Well now he has one. Hold on one second. Just wait here." Lucia ran inside and changed her shirt, went to the bathroom, quickly splashed water on her face and applied several strokes of sensual lip-gloss. She pulled her hair into a tight ponytail and went back outside. "Let's go," she said as she waved Claudia down the wheelchair ramp. The old lady rolled after her caretaker all the way to the orange Civic.

"Does this one fold up?"

"No."

She handed Claudia her cane and lifted her from the Intel chair. The ladies spun a practiced pirouette that landed Claudia in the car. She immediately fell flat left with her head landing on the driver's seat—a movement Lucia fully anticipated; neither woman reacted to it. Lucia shut the door and moved calmly to the driver's side where Claudia's head waited. She pushed Claudia upright and held her until mama could grab the blessed interior door handle. Once Claudia was situated, Lucia shoved the Intel chair into the backseat, got in and cranked the Civic into gear.

"You want your sunglasses?" Lucia asked.

The orange head banged against the glass three times. At the next stoplight Lucia leaned over and put shades on the lady who was pushed against the window like a sad fish.

"Wait 'til you see this place."

The head banged the window three more times, softer now, *yes*, *yes*, *yes*.

The Civic tottered up the long driveway. The girls' eyes got all wide—the oaks were cloaked in fiery fall fashion and knew they looked hot. They yawned overhead. "Who the hell's *that*," they asked each other, tipping their noses at the ugly rufous ride, but not *really* caring.

Lucia turned down her tunes. It's weird how the less fortunate always feel like they should be quiet in the presence of obvious wealth—though to be fair, rich people do tend to walk around like they have *very* sensitive ears.

Surprisingly, to Lucia anyway, punishing rhythm and blues licks filled the silence. She rolled down her window, saxophone and piano and drums—a lavish Sunday morning quartette for the hell of it? No, now singing, singing and piano, "But...you're *love*-lyyyyy." What the fuck? Claudia smacked the door handle and fell over onto Lucia's lap. Lucia parked and got out, the head waited. She pulled Claudia out of the car and connected her to the Intel chair.

"Wow...this is...really...really...really...something."

The piano twinkled a coy little tune from the backyard, weak yet pretty, like a fawn frightened in the road. Some people might think it better just to kill it. Others admire it and dance slowly around.

"...tearing my fear apaaaart. And that *laugh*," he giggles into the mic, "that wrinkles your nose..."

"What the fuck?" Lucia asked.

"Hello?" A gorgeous girl came striding from behind the house. The whole deal: bouncy auburn hair, round, tan and dimpled cheeks, eyelashes, eyes, perfectly petaled spring dress. Lucia could see that even the girl's toes looked beautiful.

"Hi." She had her hand out, gold bracelets jangled about her wrist—her teeth were imperfect, Lucia loved it, but realized they only enhanced her appeal.

"Hello." Lucia took the hand.

"I'm Melanie...you must be with Chef Felice's crew."

"Umm, *what?*"

"The catering? Horatio told me he'd be sending some people over to photograph the property today...so he knows, like, how much space he'll have? When he comes here next weekend to cook for...our...wedding?" Melanie sensed an evil mood developing. Upon closer examination it became quite clear that these were not members of a catering crew.

"What, because I'm Colombian, I *must* be on the catering crew?"

"I didn't mean it like that. I'm sorry."

"And what do you think *she'd* be doing? Wheeling Hors d'oeuvres around your *prahhh*-perty?"

The remnants of Melanie's summer tan grew pale. "Never, *never* change," the singer continued his feeble harmony.

"Do you even know who this is?" Lucia asked.

"I'm sorry, no...have we met?"

"No...No," Claudia slapped the armrest twice.

"This is Mrs. Salaznek."

"Keep that *breath*-less charrrrmm."

"I'm sorry?"

"Low sea you...may I please...have...a cigarette?"

Melanie shivered at the mechanical voice rising impossibly from this slackened citizen.

"Mrs. Sa-*LAZ*-nek? You know?" Lucia fumbled through her purse, pulled out a smoke, lit it up and then stuffed it between the old lady's lips. "*This*," Lucia motioned, "is Mark's mom."

"Marco's mother is dead."

"I am...alive."

"And his name is Salazar, not Salaz—whatever you said, okay? What is this about?"

"Marco changed his name—his name is Mark Salaznek. And this *is* his mom, your future mother-in-law, by the way."

"COME ON," the singer called the band back to action, trumpets and saxophone, drums, two other singers, "WOOOHOO...WOOOHOO."

Lucia lit her own cigarette and watched the precious beauty wilt as she started connecting the dots. The mute mother...the original device...the fury of LaMichael Carmichael...

"THERE'S A PARTY GOIN' ON RIGHT HERE..."

Marco turned into the driveway—lots of cars, the band, catering coming today. What a pain in the ass. He heard the band rocking from way down the driveway, "SO BRING YOUR *GOOD* TIMES, AND YOUR LAUGHTER TOOOOOO—WE GONNA CELEBRATE YOUR PARTY WITH YOU."

"Come on now, babe," Salazar finished the familiar line. His smile faded at the top of the driveway when he noticed his fiancé covered in a cloud of smoke. He saw the cute Colombian. He saw the Intel chair turning ever so slowly around—slower than slow motion, the loose skin, red dress, Claudia turned to face him, cigarette pointing from her mouth like a bit of hay. Marco's stomach dropped. When this type of social terror strikes the mind must defend itself. The brain's ability to rapidly devise unviable positive schemes in the face of utter horror is one of nature's miracles—like maybe Melanie went behind his back, found his mother (living), overlooked his hideously inhuman lie, also overlooked the incredibly sexy and voluptuous caretaker, or accepted her without any line of questioning aimed at infidelity, struck up an immediate friendship with both parties without even mentioning it to him and then invited them to the wedding and to watch rehearsal. And now they're just hanging out in the driveway taking a cigarette break.

But Melanie's wet eyes told a different story. She moved toward his car before it even stopped.

All the singers sang "CELLLLLL-UH-BRATIONNNN," as Marco opened the door. His fiancé screamed, "WHO THE FUCK ARE THESE PEOPLE, MARCO?"

The software man had not come prepared for this chaos. The Intel chair rolled his way. Lucia stood away smoking, thinking this might mark the end of her caretaking gig.

"Dead...dead...dead...dead."

"Okay Ma I got it."

"Dead...dead...dead...dead."

"So this *is* your mother?" Melanie wept, "She's alive?"

"CELLLLLL-UH-BRATIONNNN!"

"Yeah, it is. All right? So fucking *what?*"

"Dead...dead...dead...dead."

"Why would you lie about your own mother?" Melanie's bracelets jingled crazily up and down her arms. She bent at her knees as she spoke, her words more like pleas, her body begging along.

"I was embarrassed." Marco ran his fingers through his hair, which Melanie knew he did when he was nervous. He went into his black leather jacket for a cigarette, which Melanie knew he also did when he was nervous. She smacked the entire pack out of his hand and asked, "What else do you lie about...*MARK?*"

"He had...sex...with the girl...over there."

Everyone turned to look at Lucia, who smoked and waved, as she could not hear over the band, "IT'S TIME TO COME TOGETHA, IT'S UP TO YOU, WHAT'S YOUR PLEZYAA."

Melanie keeled over. Still watching, and seeing the girl drop, Lucia came running to help like a good caretaker. Melanie wasn't out long. She opened her eyes to Lucia's face and hair hanging over her. Naturally, Melanie grabbed the hair with both hands and pulled the cute Colombian on top of her. Claudia wheeled over to Marco, still pushing the "D" word on repeat. "I see that you're enjoying your new chair, Mom," he said, curling his lip.

"Dead...dead...dead...dead."

"And your new fucking floors and kitchen and ramp,

and your two-hundred-dollar-a-bottle whiskey. And *you*," he said, running to the twister of beautiful women spinning down his lawn, "the live-in nurse with a fifty thousand dollar salary for what?" He pulled Lucia off of his fiancé. "Get the fuck out of here."

"Let that cunt stay," Melanie said from the lawn, her own hair disheveled now, one of her dress straps torn and hanging. Marco had never heard her use a word on that level before. She stood up and walked over to Marco. "You *are* a fucking asshole," she said, then moved toward the garage. Marco walked after her. "I'm an asshole? I haven't done enough for everyone yet? Fuck you, Melanie," he turned, "fuck you two," he turned back, "fuck...*all* of you. Get the *fuck* outta my house then." He ran to the back of the house where the band played on. "SHUT THAT BULLSHIT DOWN RIGHT NOW. YOU GUYS BLOW, BY THE WAY." The horns fizzled out, the drums abruptly undrummed and the singer, unaware that his mic was still on, mumbled, "I told you guys that this dude hates Hispanics," to his band mates.

"Oh, I hate Hispanics?" Marco replied, being in the mood for replies. "Why don't you come around front and check out this Colombian I fucked the other night?" As the band put down their instruments, about to go check out Lucia, Melanie drove her sporty white SUV out of the garage and into the band's van that blocked her exit— they'd backed all the way in, nose in front of the garage, to make unloading the equipment easier. The path did not become totally clear with the initial impact, so Melanie pushed harder on the accelerator. As the van was in park, the tires were locked. So instead of just sliding over to allow Melanie's exit, the van started to tilt.

"This bitch is nuts," Lucia said to Claudia. "I think I love her."

"Dude, *STOP*," yelled the drummer, then did that thing people in crisis are always doing. "That's our van!" As if who owned the van made any difference to Melanie—as if

Melanie, who invited the band there and helped them set up, wasn't already totally aware whose van she was ramming.

Well, that van (owned by the band) did eventually flop over on its side. Glass crunched and slid out from underneath like the internal organs of a jumper. Melanie had not considered what might happen to her intensely revving car once it wiggled free—she took off like a rocket, not straight down the paved path either. The dented grill pointed for one of the thick oaks lining the driveway. She swerved back the other way to avoid the tree, but overreacted and ended up bouncing over the small hill that separated lawn from driveway. She screamed a bit inside the car as it careened down the stately lawn— the stunned onlookers were *stunned*. This was quite a departure from traditional Brookville behavior. Claudia's cigarette fell from her mouth and started to work its way through her red dress.

"Go GUUUURL," Lucia shouted, as the band checked out her ass, which did pleasantly distract them from their wrecked vehicle.

Melanie again overcompensated, too desperate to regain the driveway. She could have calmly applied the brake and stopped on the lawn—this is the shit sport utility vehicles were designed for. They can handle lawns, carpools to school, mud, snow, ski trips, rain and ice. They cannot handle a maniac spinning the wheel like it's an insane game show. The sporty white SUV traveled decently far on two tires before it flipped over and destroyed Marco's lawn. Given his mood, Marco first thought of his landscape artist who would really earn his pay this autumn. Then he thought of his fiancé, who he loved more than anything, banging around inside the SUV. He prayed that she had remembered to buckle her safety belt—he'd picked that car for her because the car-selling artist said, "This is the absolute safest car on the road today. Bulletproof stuff. Steel everything. Airbags *everywhere.*" But despite the way some people act, there is no human on earth too tough for a seatbelt. You can also be sure that any consistently unbuckled person will have major issues other than blatant disregard for personal safety.

Thankfully, Melanie still cared about her life—she had buckled up—knocked out and bloody when everyone got to her, but totally alive. Seizing what he thought to be an opportunity, one of the band members jumped onto the SUV, which rested on its passenger side. He pulled Melanie's door open, fighting gravity, and of course asked, "Are you all right?" But she was knocked out so she didn't answer. Then the band member, in loafers, khakis and a plain blue button front (short sleeve), yelled, "She's bleeding!" and dipped his torso into the car in an attempt to unhook the seatbelt—airbags were everywhere. Now Marco jumped onto the car. He'd discarded his leather jacket while running down the lawn and did look like a hero with his black hair all over his face and his tan muscles bulging from his white V-neck T-shirt.

He pulled the band man out of the car first: "Dude if you unbuckle her seatbelt now she's gonna fall down into the car. She might have a neck injury." Again, very clear that Marco Salazar is the smartest guy on the scene. He flung the band member back down onto the lawn and politely asked the band to go home. The band politely responded that their means of transportation lay in ruins just up the driveway.

Salazar turned his attention to the damsel in distress. "Baby...baby are you okay?" he asked. She didn't respond, but Marco noticed movement in her eyelids. He caressed her cheek and sat on the overturned car until the ambulance arrived.

"What the hell happened here?" asked a reasonably interested EMS guy. His eyes not on Melanie but scanning the chaotically torn up lawn, *two* flipped vehicles, stunning chain-smoking Colombian, band on standby and computerized elderly woman with smoke coming from her underpants.

"Nothing," Marco replied, motioning for them to just get on with saving his fiancé.

It took three men to free Melanie from the SUV—one to stabilize her neck, one to hold her body, and one to cut the seatbelt. As she stared up at the bright sky from a stretcher, blood on her face and glass in her hair, she decided she'd prefer not to come back to this place. Marco's voice, *Mark's* voice, attempting to calm her and apologize, produced instead an adverse reaction, and she puked onto the lawn. The EMS guy said, "Looks like her neck's okay." Marco thought he might smash this guy's nose in for him.

The bastards wouldn't let Marco into the ambulance either. Said his presence is clearly upsetting to the girl.

In the hospital the nurse told him, "The patient doesn't want to see you."

Her parents walked through the waiting area without a word.

He stayed overnight.

He tried to sleep in the perpendicular waiting area chairs—stiff enough to make you think of dead bodies, anything but comforting.

He drank hospital coffee.

He read hospital magazines.

People.

Bizarre.

Life.

National Geographic.

He ate the brown-green food.

She walked out, slightly crying, parents at either side—Mother's arm around daughter.

"Melanie, please," he begged.

Mother and daughter continued onward.

Father stayed behind for a quick chat. He pointed to Marco's chin. "If you *ever*..." you know, "come near *MY* daughter again..."

Salazar wasn't havin' it. The last thing he wanted to see was this dude's face in his face. This guy who didn't offer a penny for the wedding—who asked his own daughter to ask her boyfriend if he'd get her parents a Caribbean cruise for Christmas, who wanted to fly first class to Miami to board that Caribbean cruise and who, upon returning from that cruise, never said 'thanks so much for the trip, Marco' but complained about overcooked steak and sea sickness and flight delays for two entire dinners, which Marco also generously funded without complaint because he loved this dude's daughter.

"What are you gonna do? Huh?" Marco asked, shoving the man through those flapping hospital doors.

"You better watch yourself, boy," the man cautioned.

Marco didn't like his tone and unloaded. He tossed him over the front curb and onto his ass there in the paved pickup area. Looking real embarrassed, the man went to get up off his ass but Salazar flew from the curb, cocked back and blasted him in the lip, just above the jaw—Marco could feel father's tooth come through the lip. Blood sprayed in every direction as the man's head smashed against the pavement. When father went to shield his face with shaking hands, Marco took him up by his gray hair— his gray wig, it pulled away from his bald head and so revealed marvelously consistent rows of red patchwork dots up and down the otherwise shiny scalp. Bits of remaining hair and glue also distorted the shininess. The man, free of his hair, fell flat on the ground and grabbed at his face. Blood and tears streamed down his cheeks. Marco examined the freshly detached shag. He laughed and wanted to sniff at it but two police officers came jiggling out of the hospital. He threw father's hair back to him. The cops grabbed his hands and pulled out the cuffs. Marco spun around with his elbows, gave them the, "Do you know who I am?" But it didn't work—it almost never works, it's not worth trying. If they knew who you were, you wouldn't have to ask.

"You're fucked, you're both totally fucked." He kicked like a baby, not getting his way. "Do you know who I am? Do you know who I am? Do you know who I am?"

18

$\mathcal{A}$ plastic Santa stood, unlit, looking over the Dwarf Alberta—arms folded as though he'd just planted the thing. Santa's face glazed and waxy with ice, he looked like the largest holiday cookie ever baked. Two strands of Christmas lights (also unlit) ran up both rails of the wheelchair ramp to Kringle's rear. People who use these multicolored lights, instead of white, are often the same people who leave their lights out into late February.

The giant bus buzzed in front of the house. Energetic silhouettes moved back and forth and up and down behind the foggy windows. Smoke fumed visibly into the frozen night, rising to join the neighborhood's billowing chimneys. Tiny Patchogue puffed eternally into the sky, faintly recalling the height of American industry. Power wires and telephone wires cut through the blue-gray fog like staffs of Selene's sheet music. Jagged moonlit chips flaked down and strengthened the uniform slippery army that choked all roads.

"So, who are *you*?"

"I work at Egostatistical, for Marco Salazar...you see, he's having this huge work party at his house to celebrate the número uno buyout, ya know? And I'm the only one who didn't get invited."

"How do you know?"

"It's because I'm Hispanic."

"How do you know?"

"Well, he hates Hispanics."

"No, Jesus, I mean...how do you know you're the only one who wasn't invited?"

"I checked a co-workers email."

The little *chorlito* stood shaking at the front door, his winter cap draped loosely over his ears. He looked Lucia over to the point of examining. His stale sangria breath made her sick.

"So why are you *here,* then?"

"We told *that* guy," he pointed to the street, at Boyle, "to bring us to Marco Salazar's...and he brought us here."

"That makes sense," Lucia said, "this is his mom's house. Marco grew up here."

"He grew up *here?*"

"Yep. Right here. You should have seen it before."

Lucia invited the freezing weasel into the house.

"So I take it he didn't invite you to the party either?"

"I don't work there."

"Yeah, but you work *for* him, right?"

"I do. But the last time we went over there things got a little out of hand. We actually haven't heard from Marco in months."

The magic escalator chair clicked to life from the top of the stairs. The weasel jerked his head almost backwards, like an owl but much quicker. He pulled his collar. "What's that?" Lucia didn't answer. They waited together—first the right foot, leg, shoulder came into view, bits of the stiff orange hair peeking, right cheek, right hand with bottle, wool sweater almost the size of her body, jeans tucked into wool socks. Then her left side emerged from behind the wall, frowning in totality. Lucia went to her and hooked her up to the Intel chair.

"Who is...this...tiny man?"

"Hello, Mrs. Salazar, my name is Jorge." He got up and stuck out his hand, awkwardly, realizing a handshake might be impossible, given the bottle, maybe even inappropriate, given the left hand.

"My name...is...sull...lass...neck."

"Actually, her name is Salaznek. We can't figure out how to make it do names."

"What?" asked the weasel.

"And Marco is really Mark. He changed his name."

"So you must know where he lives then."

"We do."

"Do you wanna crash this party with us?"

Claudia Salaznek pounded her bottle on the armrest three times.

*   *   *

*M*arco looked down at the ice that encased all his garage doors. Six, seven, maybe eight inches of it—the word 'thick' could not be ignored, the word *pickax* the only eligible reply. And even then, pickax in hand(s), plunging the tundra, the affair would last hours. How even to purchase a pickax? A tool designated for tradesmen. Marco's sharp features and cutting eyes suggested executive. You just can't bring it to the register nonchalantly; he'd have to invent an excuse: "Surely, you never know when you might be trapped in a Glaze Event." The register artist hands over the change. The word 'murderer' flashes through his or her mind, but she or he remains silent, not wanting to upset the wealthy looking customer.

He kicked the ice bashfully, shucks, holding only a plastic shovel—and not even that powerful rocket kind of plastic. This baby was made from the plastic that bends. A harsh wind taunted the software man. "Come onnn big boyyy, give 'er a tryyy..." The freeze bit his exposed skin, now the color of a cadaver, and his bones just as cold.

The orange shovelhead looked scared, the yellow shaft weak. Marco felt nothing more than an insignificant dark dot surrounded by the great estate that slashed wide diamond smears in every direction. Innumerable tree limbs lay perverted and inky, scattered about the bleached lawn—felled silent victims, twisted and still, attest to Wanda's demon wrath.

But this hot young software man had overcome greater odds in his time—what's a little ice to a guy that had grown up cleaning shit off the floor? It all goes away, anything can be cleared—you just have to start.

And so he started with the wedge technique. He battered the tough surface, holding his weapon horizontally, chopping down, hoping to create a gap where ice meets garage door. But the ever-so-slightly rounded arc of the shovelhead would not allow for the precise angle necessary to strike the exact meeting place—it wouldn't do any good to chip away at the ice, even an inch in front of the door. Marco dropped to one knee to achieve the proper angle of attack. He flipped his furry hood from his head so he could see. Falling ice snippets clung to every tip of his wool hat like static. He stabbed the shovelhead into the ice, crack-crack-crack. Again, crack-crack-crack, he tried to work, to be efficient and dedicated, but the ice cascaded down. Wind whipped ruthlessly all around the estate. The terrible unending howl sent the precipitation spiraling in irregular waves. Marco knelt lower. Trying to use the back half of the black beast as protection, he kept working, crack-crack-crack.

* * *

Lucia squeezed the handles at the back of the chair, taking great care not to let go or slip on the icy ramp. The weasel, to his credit, braced the front of the chair with admirable and astounding athleticism—he held Claudia's shins and backpedaled (on his *knees*) down the frozen ramp saying, "Thatta girl, that's a girl, great, you're doing great." To the weasel's discredit, he didn't give a shit about Claudia reconnecting with her son, or whatever he told them—he wanted her for the added embarrassment her presence would cause when they all showed up at the party. He'd have proof that *Mark* really was a selfish asshole—look at all these poor people, and look, he disowned his own mother. Yeah, see what you get for not inviting Jorge to the party?

Several 2s got off the bus to help carry Claudia down the slick driveway and out to the road. First they thought they'd leave her in the chair, but this was kind of impossible because they had nothing to grip but the wheels, which spun, and when she spilled out onto the driveway (along with her whiskey), they decided it would be better for Lucia to take the chair to the bus separately—after running inside to fetch a new bottle. With a man stationed at each limb, and two more on the torso, six 2s inched Claudia Salaznek down her mostly flat driveway. They shuffled cautiously, baby steps. As the sharp precipitation stung the woman's face, she shut her eyes, "Goin' to uhh partayyyyy," she thought, but could not say.

Those still on the bus opened all the windows so she could hear their encouraging cheers. Boyle moved down the aisle. They cheered. He heaved open the large yellow swinging rear door. They cheered. He walked back up the aisle to his seat and engaged the motorized elevator that loaded sweet Claudia into the bus. They cheered. Lucia circled to the front and entered through the folding doors. Boyle asked, "Goin' somewhere?" And she told him where to go. Boyle shifted into gear and they cheered. They offered Claudia some sangria. She took it and passed her fresh whiskey. They cheered, passed the whiskey.

Ancient thick trees toppled like dominoes around him, seemingly getting closer all the time. The software man, standing tall in his boots and re-hooded, attacked with his entire arsenal—kicking feet, punching hands, shovelhead, shovel handle. When he made a dent he bent over and pulled with his gloved fingers. It did not take a hoodless owl to notice the glorious eighteen by three (inch) trench Marco had carved at the extreme left of his garage door (the side closest to the protruding black beast). So that's a foot and a half...and halfway down...on a nine-foot wide door, in hardly an hour. As he smashed the orange shovelhead into the fresh trench he truly believed that reaching the ground, creating this eighteen-inch long hole, would allow him to clear the rest of the ice with relative ease. He could get right down *in there* and employ the side of the shovelhead with a chopping axe motion to the exposed corner. When he got tired of axing he would heel the shit out of it, stomping away with a landing area and a bit of exposed driveway for hope and inspiration. He just needed to meet that initial goal—Marco dreamed of driveway, wanted to shout Land, ho!

His pace quickened—crack-crack-crack, crackcrack-crackcrack. Every earth-shattering stab rose from some bottomless dark pit within this man who would not be contained—he struck with a force set to impale, his mind ran red against invisible adversaries. The jacket over his mouth, frozen stiff from breath and spit, cut blue lines into his chin—battle scars, crusty blood. He could hear his heart pounding inside the hood. He plunged the tool down with the ferocity, pride and style of a nearly victorious Renaissance knight.

YES.

YES.

YES.

Oh how the smallest bits of ice splattered. The trench got deeper, easier to dig at increasing depths. Wanda's vise grip weakened and dreams of Ohekan orgies danced through his head, crackcrack-crackcrack...CRACK.

The orange shovelhead split up the middle—much like the garage door to Marco's left. He pondered the plastic disaster for a moment then Micky Mantled it into the garage door, WHACK and WHACK. Unsatisfied, he turned the shovelhead upon the black beast and with just one strike on the rugged steel the shovelhead went flying into the night—a comet or shooting star, so pretty, totally detached from shaft and handle. Salazar now examined his new weapon, calling it, "You fucking plastic piece of shit." And yet he admired the fresh jagged edge at the end of the shaft. It looked deadly, like a blessing. He took it up above his head to a height that tested his torso's flexibility. He put the force of his entire body behind the sharp spear and stabbed the frozen ground. Up again. Down again went this pathetic bayonet—Salazar's brain too frozen to see that Wanda refilled the trench as he worked. The unfulfilling dash of sunny color rose into the sable sky and plunged toward the ivory earth like the forlorn filter of some failed photographer, something so incredibly mediocre that it makes you sad and so becomes a work of art.

Marco's final stab turned catastrophic. His right foot slipped backward on the ice just as he started his downward motion. The angry momentum sent him reeling to the tundra at breakneck speed. He lowered his hands, braced for impact, but his right wrist could not bear the weight and snapped like all those far-off tree limbs, from close proximity the sound was disturbingly similar. With the wrist giving way nothing could prevent his head from smashing onto the ice. It went kaboom.

Black.

Stars.

Ice.

Ice gnashing ice—Selene's eternal tune twinkled to earth. The freakish confetti burned into his eyes as he stared at the colorless sky—a blurry collage of white noise and static TVs of yore. Marco gripped his wrist, "Ahhhh," tried to sit up. Too dizzy. Too slippery. Lights coming up the road? Noise?

"WE'RE NUMBER ONE. WE'RE NUMBER ONE. *SOMOS EL NÚMERO UNO.*"

"The wheels on the bus go buzz-buzz-buzz, buzz-buzz-buzz...ALLLLLL THROUGH THE TOWNNNNNN."

"YO...holy *shit*, mang. Look at that, this is my kinda party."

"What?" Jorge asked.

"Ju don't see that, mang? There's a giant truck sticking out the damn garage."

They cheered.

Lights coming up the driveway. Why? Who? The wheels on the bus go buzz-buzz-buzz, all through the town. Boyle. Boyle's bus. Why?

"There he is." Jorge pointed at Marco Salazar.

Marco rolled closer to the garage door and used his left hand to stabilize himself. He stood up, covered in everything. The falling ice came into focus. He blinked. The bus parked. The doors unfolded and let out a tiny man who shimmied like a drunken duckling toward Marco.

"George?"

"My name's Jorge, motherfucker."

The 2s filed from the bus. The back door unlatched and flapped open. Marco heard the elevator's mechanical sound, saw glints of sparkling rims lowered to the driveway.

"Juan Miguel?"

"I told you this wasn't over, mang."

"What are you guys doing here?"

"We came to join the fiesta," Jorge replied.

"What?"

"Don't play stupid...*Mark*. I read the email."

Salazar couldn't believe his ears. "I cancelled the party, you dumb fuck. Look around...do you even see *one* car—do you hear any people? Can you find a single light on inside my house?"

Jorge took a moment to survey the scene. The large arc of 2s behind him acknowledged that the software man had a point.

"Don't ju talk to Jorge like that," Juan Miguel said.

Claudia wheeled around from the back of the bus, "Dead...dead...dead...dead."

Marco's wrist pulsated. He could feel it swelling against his increasingly tight wool sweater. Even with her winter cap on he could see Claudia's rotting flesh sliding from her skull, whiskey bottle in the cup holder to her right—Lucia jabbed a lit cigarette into the woman's mouth. For the first time in his life Marco wished that Claudia *had* died in their driveway that day. For the first time in his life he blamed her. He blamed her for all the fury stored within him and for his inability to truly enjoy anything without thinking of the awful plague that stained his life—the only thing he could not erase or change. He watched her smoke, knew she smiled inside. "Dead...dead...dead...dead." She pushed the button again and again. The force of her entire being exhaled into the air and looked at her son through the lone good eye. The 2s stood silently aside but rocked noticeably from heel to toe. Claudia's anger seemed to heat them. They oscillated strangely, ready to boil.

"What the *fuck* do you want?" Marco shouted at all the uninvited.

Juan Miguel answered with a vicious ice ball to the software man's gorgeous face. Marco stumbled back against the garage. He tried to pick up the shovel shaft to defend himself but his right hand, his default, wouldn't work. He let a painful moan die against his jacket collar. The 2s all jumped in at the weasel's behest. They trapped him against the garage. They kicked and stomped and yelled. Boyle watched from behind the bus windshield, his mouth downed in disbelief—his headlights spotlighting the scene. Stone wasn't coming. Hurricane Schwartz nowhere in sight. Sangria bottles flew through windows and smashed against the brick façade above the garage.

The glass fell on top of Marco who squirmed helpless, like a spider in water, as the 2s kicked the living shit out of him. They pummeled poor Marco in that way you're completely desensitized to. You're not thinking about what it tastes like when your lip gets stomped so hard two teeth come through, or how quickly all that blood freezes, or the burning sensation beneath the eyes when someone's nose gets flattened and how hard breathing becomes. How many times must you see someone beaten before you get to wondering about the pain? He tries to yell but is silenced by the heel. He begs. You should think about that person—begging, voiceless. What's it like to get labeled straight away? Most of the 2s throwing bottles through the windows of the black beast knew nothing of the man sprawled out there on the ground—but they heard he said a bad thing once, changed his name, disowned his mother. And now swept into this massive tidal wave polluted by popular opinion they figure let's ride this bitch to shore. There's nowhere else to go.

The End
is near.
Para la Fiesta, apretar el dos.

Looky here—somewhere else to go. Would you believe it? Well believe it, I did it for you. I'm giving you this option, this...possibility. I have to—I don't want to be a hypocrite. Now just imagine this for a moment: The 2s pull up and see Marco lying there. They recognize him as one human and they show human concern. They bring him inside and realize the party has in fact been cancelled. But they figure, since we're all here, we might as well have a new party—hell, it beats beating the shit out of each other right? Marco points the 2s toward the wine cellar and relights all his dynamic candles. The house smells delicious. All the bodies make it warm. They speak to each other and decide they've got more in common than reddening teeth. They dance and sing in the twinkling candlelight. They smoke and laugh as Claudia drives her wheelchair in circles in the middle of an impromptu dance floor. She raises a right-handed salute. The power comes back. The entire world is open to them now. She's dancing. The sangria slams and falls in her hair. Her son towels her once again. Call it what you want. Call it dancing. Call it happiness. It's your choice. It's your gift. The runway is clear—takeoff.

www.ingramcontent.com/pod-product-compliance
Lightning Source LLC
Chambersburg PA
CBHW051122260626
47170CB00005B/1614